# The Girl with the Broken Smile

## By: Lindsay Paige

*To My Mommala,*

*Who always wanted me to be a lawyer. Look at me now.*

# Chapter 1: Semi-Charmed Life

When you are born dead, everything is kind of uphill from there. But how can you be born dead? Well, maybe I should start by explaining my oxymoron. On July 24th, 1986, my beautiful mother, Nancy Arlene Young, gave birth to a 6lb 8oz dead baby girl. According to my mother's recollection, when the doctor pulled me out, I wasn't breathing because I had shit inside the womb and swallowed it, so basically, I accomplished the literal interpretation of eat shit and die. The doctors and nurses surrounded me as they sucked the shit out of my lungs and brought me back to life. And so, it was the beginning of my lovely life journey.

"Can I see my baby?" My mother pleaded.

"I don't know if you want to." Said the doctor.

"Why the fuck not?" She replied.

She had such a way with words, my mother, but we'll get to that later.

The doctor hesitated as he took me over to her.

"You see Ms. Young, she has, well, a hair lip."

Great. Not only was I dead, but I was also deformed. This is shaping up to be a wonderful story.

"Give me my goddamn baby!" She yelled as she snatched me from his arms.

She looked at me and ran her fingers through my auburn hair.

"You are the most beautiful baby in the world. Your mommy is going to take care of you and protect you from any harm." She whispered as she kissed the opening of my upper lip.

My parents immediately searched high and low for the best cleft lip and palate pediatric plastic surgeon in America. That is when they found Dr. Marsh at Children's Hospital in St. Louis, MO. He was the best of the best, specializing in cleft lip/palate and cranial facial deformities. They were able to get a referral from my pediatrician but needed help in financing my many years of plastic surgery.

Depending on the severity of the deformity, cleft lip and palate patients could end up having 10-15 surgeries during their childhood.

My dad had insurance through his work, but the bills were going to astronomical.

"Well, the Ronald McDonald House turned us down." My dad said as he slammed the letter down on the kitchen table in from of my mom.

"Turned us down? Why?" She asked infuriated.

"I make too much money." He responded.

"That mother fucking piece of shit clown ass bitch! I will roll up to his Ronald McDonald House and light that bitch on fire, clown shoes and all." She yelled.

"We'll find a way to pay for her surgeries." My dad said as he comforted her.

And by some miracle, or the by the grace of God himself, my dad's insurance approved my first surgery and they were able to finance the rest.

Being a baby pretty much sucked for me. I went into my first surgery at six weeks old to close the hole in my lip. Fixing my lip was the easy part, the hardest part of this journey was going to be the palate surgeries because it affected my facial development and speech.

Besides my parents and the medical staff, none of my other family members wanted to touch me, especially during bottle time. Because of the cleft palate, I couldn't breast fead and I had to feed from a special bottle with a long nipple that basically shot the milk straight down my throat. This process terrified everyone because it always sounded like I was choking, which I probably was, but who wouldn't want to just end it all right then and there?

If it were not for my mother, I would never have been picked up or loved on because everyone was scared of hurting me. But being a complete and utter optimist, even back then, it did not hinder me from being a happy baby. I was always smiling, even though my smile was broken.

After my first palate surgery, my parents were given the green light to feed me solid foods and I didn't waste any time making up for my lack of sustenance months prior. I went from the skinniest baby to the fattest baby overnight; my love of food that would maturate over the years and bring me unsolicited weight gain, but that's a different story for a different day.

My family and I moved around quite a bit during my early childhood years from my birthplace of Cape Girardeau, Missouri to Memphis, Tennessee, and eventually to Wingate, NC, a suburb of Charlotte. My dad was an engineer with a short fuse deemed in one of his annual evaluations as, "difficult to work with". Because of that, he went from job-to-job and we went along for the ride. I thought it was normal not to live in one place for a long period of time, so I didn't mind it.

Some of my first memories were from living in North Carolina. We had the perfect American house with the two kids and a dog, Angie our Cocker Spaniel. I just remember going on adventures into the woods behind our house with the neighborhood kids and not having any care in the world, even though I probably should have.

Back in the late 1980s and early 1990s, there was a slew of kidnappings across the country; PSAs on the television about kids should not talk to strangers, never realizing that it could actually happen to me, but it did. Yes, I was kidnapped. Obviously, everything turned out okay, otherwise, I wouldn't be writing this right now, but it was quite the experience.

My parents decided to take my brother and me one Saturday to the Eastland mall just outside of Charlotte to go to the pet store to see puppies. My dad was looking after my brother and my mom pushed me in the stroller. My mom turned her back while she was looking at puppies, but when she turned around, I was gone. I was only two years old at the time and don't remember much, but I do remember a man carrying me in the mall and me screaming, "you're not my mommy!" at the top of my lungs. My screams couldn't be ignored and must have scared my abductor so much that he literally dropped me in front of JCPenney and ran off. I didn't know where I was, but I saw a bunch of clothes, stumbled upon a dressing room, and started to play dress-up. I was busy trying on bras when I heard a woman yell, "She's in here! I found her!".

My mom was beside herself with fear and joy because she knew that the situation could have had a much different and tragic outcome. But before you call me lucky, that was only the beginning of the string of bad luck and unfortunate events that took place during my childhood.

My family and I were in the process of moving, yet again, but we needed to stay at my grandparent's house in Blodgett, MO until we were able to find a new home. We moved in a lot of our personal belongings, clothes, books, pictures, and our animals (our beloved Angie, two Persian kittens, and a Shar-Pei puppy).

"I am taking the kids into town to run errands; do you want me to take Drew too?" My mom asked my aunt Penny.

"I forgot his car seat; I have to go back to the house to get it." She replied.

"Well aren't you a dumb ass. I guess he can just stay here with dad and granny Lambert." My mom said in frustration.

My cousin Drew was only a few months old and since my aunt forgot his car seat, my grandpa and great grandma decided to babysit him while my aunt went to work.

My mom piled up my brother, my cousin Ted, and myself in the car and went into town to run errands. On our way back, my mom saw cop car lights behind her and thought she was getting pulled over, but the cop sped past us.

"Where's the fire?" She said jokingly.

When we got closer, we could see the billowing clouds of smoke. There was an actual fire.

"Oh my god, I hope it isn't our house, please god say it isn't our house." My mom kept saying out loud. As she drove closer, she knew that it was.

She stopped the car, ran out as fast as she could trying to get into the house, but it was engulfed in flames.

"Drew! Drew!" She yelled because she knew my baby cousin was in the house when we left.

A firefighter swooped her up in his arms preventing her from trying to go into the house as she tried to fight him off.

My grandpa walked up to her with his oxygen tank (he suffered from Emphysema) and she yelled, "Where the fuck is Drew? Where is he?"

"He is at Granny Lambert's house; she took him over there as soon as we got out." He said as my mom began to cry in relief. My Granny Lambert's house was adjacent to my grandparent's house.

"And Angie?" She asked my grandpa.

"Honey, I'm so sorry. I got her out and had her by the collar, but she heard the puppy crying and ran back into the house. I tried to go back in to get her, but the fire was too strong." Said, my grandpa.

That's when I saw my mom truly lose it. Up until that point in my life, I had seen my mom sad, especially whenever I went in for surgery, but I had never seen her have a complete mental breakdown and it was terrifying.

My brother, cousin, and I were still in the car watching all of this unfold right before our eyes. I looked up at the top window of the burning house and I could see one of our Persian cats clawing at the window to get out, but there was nothing anyone could do.

In one single day, we lost everything we owned and became homeless.

Thankfully, with the help of the community and the assistance of The Salvation Army, we were provided with the essentials like clothing, food, etc.

My dad received a job offer from an engineering company in Chicago, IL, so he decided to move us all into a tiny hotel room on the outskirts of the city.

Being a little kid, I thought that living in a hotel room was the coolest thing ever and I had no idea how bad or dire our situation truly was. We got to play around in a hotel like Danny in The Shining, minus the psychotic father. The hotel had an indoor pool, so that was where I received some of my first swimming lessons, and near-drowning experiences as well.

One certain day my mom brought my brother and me to the pool for us to swim while she read the latest celebrity gossip magazine. My brother wanted me to swim over to him in the deep end of the pool, which I had never done before, but I felt brave enough to try it out that day.

Meanwhile, my mom was interrupted by a young and handsome man.

"Are you here visiting?" He asked her.

She looked up from her magazine and said, "No, living here temporarily until we find a house."

"We?" He asked.

"Yeah, my kids and I." She said as she pointed over to my brother and me.

"Oh, nice! My friend and I are here for a wedding this weekend. His daughter is getting married." He said as he checked her out.

I'm not going to lie; my mom was a hottie. She was 5'2", 100 lbs, and short red hair. She received a lot of attention from men and she was a natural flirt.

"That's nice." She said as she buried her head back into the magazine.

"What are you planning on doing today?" He asked trying to keep up the conversation.

"Oh, the kids want to go to the movies. My daughter is obsessed with Johnny Depp, so we're going to see Edward Scissorhands."

Little did she know, because she was too busy flirting, but I was struggling to stay afloat at the deep end of the pool.

"Isn't that a little scary for little kids? Why don't you take them to see my movie?" He asked.

My mom laughed, "Your movie? And what would that be?"

"Home Alone." He responded seriously.

"Home Alone? You made that movie?" She said still laughing.

Then she looked over at the seat next to the handsome gentleman she was flirting with and saw actor Peter Boyle.

She looked back at the guy and he stuck out his hand and said, "Hi I'm Chris, nice to meet you."

She was freaking flirting with director Chris Columbus who not only directed the classic Home Alone, but also Gremlins, Mrs. Doubtfire, and Harry Potter.

"Mom! Lindsay's drowning", my brother said as he ran up to her.

My mom looked down at the end of the pool and I was wailing my arms and finally went under.

Finally, this is it, this is the end of what I tried to finish when I was born. This was finally my time to go.

Then I felt a hand grab my arm and pull me up.

"What the fuck is your problem? I can't leave you alone for two seconds and you drown? C'mon." She said with such concern as she grabbed me and my brother and left the pool area.

"Nice to meet you! Have fun at Edward Scissorhands!", yelled Chris.


Living in the suburbs of Chicago was great; I felt like every John Hughes character all wrapped into one. We lived there when Michael Jordan and the Chicago Bulls reigned supreme; my friends at school were huge Jordan fans, but I was obsessed with Dennis Rodman. He was cool, he was a little crazy, and you could never predict what he was going to do next. I think the main reason why I liked him was that he was different than any other basketball player at that time, something that I could relate to as well.

It was around this time when my mom felt it necessary to be more involved in school activities; I guess being a stay-at-home mom wasn't very stimulating and she was a very vivacious person who needed interaction with others.

She encouraged me to sign up for the Girl Scouts of America as a Brownie Scout. Now, even at such a young age I wasn't much for joining group organizations, but all of my friends in my class were in it and I wanted to be liked so bad, so I joined.

My mom willingly volunteered herself as a troop leader which made me insanely jealous. All of the little girls in my troop loved my mom and wanted to cling onto her like animals in the wild; I didn't get it; didn't they have their own moms to fawn over? After a year of being a Scout, I begged my mom to quit and she finally agreed, but only if she and I went on the annual retreat in the woods together.

Not only did I hate organized groups, but I hated organized groups who congregated in the damn forest. Being the girly girl that I was, the thought of sleeping in a cabin in the woods, in the middle of winter in Illinois was not my cup of tea.

"Oh c'mon Linz, it'll be fun. Just you and I hanging out in the woods together." My mom said as she zipped up my second coat layer before we boarded the bus.

"It doesn't sound like fun to me." I said as I pouted.

"Well, you're no daughter of mine. Dooon't like being out in the wilderness, fending for yourself." She replied.

She used to always say stuff like that to me. I guess she wanted me to be more like her. When she was young, she used to be outside all day long, walking up and down the train tracks near her house, talking to vagabonds who just hopped off the train. I was more of a modern girl who loved nice things like indoor plumbing and heat.

My mom and I boarded the bus with the other girls ready for an adventure.

When we arrived, the owner of the camp greeted us and gave us a tour of the place. It looked like Camp Crystal Lake had a fire, a hurricane, and an earthquake all at once. The place was terrifying.

"And let me show you your bathroom." Said the tour guide as she guided us outside.

"We're going to have to shit in the woods?" I asked.

"Lindsay watch your mouth!" My mom exclaimed.

Might I mention that I cussed, a lot. It was pretty much the only thing I used to get in trouble for, but I couldn't stop. I used to tell my mom I thought I had Turrets, but she knew where I got my potty mouth from.

"No, not exactly. You have an outhouse!" Said the guide as she opened the door to my biggest nightmare.

I looked at my mom and she was smiling so big; she loved this. It was like some sort of sick torture for her to make me freak out.

"No, there is no way I'm going to the bathroom in there. What if I have to go at night?" I asked.

"Take a flashlight and watch out for Black Widows that will crawl up and bite you in your ass." My mom said laughing.

I could start to feel the tears well up in my eyes as we finished the tour.

"We all made a cleaning and cooking schedule for everyone over the weekend, so make sure to take a look to see when you're scheduled." Another troop mom announced.

My mom looked over at me and rolled her eyes which made me laugh.

"Is something funny Lindsay?" She asked.

"No ma'am", I replied as I looked back at my mom who was laughing harder.

We all ate dinner together, cooked by another troop mom and her daughter, and my mom and I had the chore of cleaning up after everyone.

After dinner, my mom and I got situated in our cabin and were getting ready for bed.

"Why are you not underneath the covers?" She asked.

"Ew, there is no telling what's in those. I refuse." I said disgusted by the thought.

"Suit yourself, it's going to be cold tonight." My mom replied.

Later that night my eyes popped open when I felt a huge urge to purge. Maybe it was the dirty hot dogs we ate for dinner or maybe it was the pure disgust of the environment, but my stomach was tossing and turning as I could feel the chunks start to rise.

"Mom! Mom!" I whispered trying to wake her up.

Then, I was at the point of no return. I had to make a run for it outside.

As soon as I stepped out into the cold air, I could feel the vomit spew out of my mouth. Once I stopped, relief consumed my entire body. What was it about the aftermath of a good throw-up? You always feel a thousand times better once you release the demons from your body. I breathed a sigh of relief and thought to myself, that wasn't so bad. But as fast as that thought escaped my mind, I could feel the rumbling begin in my gut and the instant pain. I had to shit, and I had to shit right then. A wave of panic, or maybe it was the shit pains, sent a shockwave in my system as I looked over at the outhouse. There was no way in hell I was going in there, even if it was to lose my colon. It was dark and cold, and I left my flashlight in the cabin in my hurry to hurl.

I had no other choice; I had to face my fears and go into the outhouse. It was coming and it was coming fast. I used the sleeve of my nightgown to open the door and the smell made me want to vomit all over again. I pulled my underwear down as I hovered over the toilet area and let it go. I used my foot to keep the door cracked for what it felt like forever. Once I was finished, I took a sigh of relief, looked down, and saw that there was no toilet paper.

"Son of a bitch!" I yelled.

It was such a mess because I had hovered, so some of it splashed up on me. I couldn't use my nightgown sleeve because, well, that's just freaking gross. So, I did what anyone else would have done. I ran out of the outhouse, bare-assed and into the opening of the woods to find a leaf. I found a good pile and squatted down to wipe when I felt a sting on my ass. I had just been bitten by something. I pulled my underwear up and ran back to my cabin as fast as I could crying. Not crying because I was hurt, but because of what my mom was going to do.

"Mom! Mom!" I yelled crying.

"What? What?" She asked waking up.

"I was just bit by something outside," I said crying.

"Outside, what the hell were you doing outside?" She yelled.

"I got sick and had to throw up and I got bit by something," I said, leaving out my shit story.

She got out of bed and turned on the light.

"Oh my god, you have hives!" She yelled as I looked down and saw the huge welts all over my body.

"Come here, I brought some Benadryl." She said as she went over to her bag and pulled out the pill form of Benadryl.

"You know I can't swallow pills", I said crying.

"Well, you're going to learn today." She said as she got a glass of water and put two pills in my hand.

"Throw those in the back of your throat, take a sip of water, and swallow." She said as she handed me the glass of water.

Tears were running down my face as my face was swelling up; I placed the two pills in the back of my throat and started choking.

"Goddammit Lindsay, just take a sip of water, it's not that hard", my mom yelled.

"I'm trying", I said sobbing.

I tried it again, but with water this time, and spit out the pills.

"Get over here!" My mom said as she grabbed the pills, opened my mouth, and shoved them down my throat.

"Drink!" She yelled as she shoved the glass of water in my face.

I took a drink and the pills finally went down.

We both sat on the bed not saying anything to each other.

"You have a death wish, don't you?" She asked.

I didn't say anything back to her, maybe it was because of the trauma of the evening or because my tongue swelled up and I couldn't.

We just sat there in silence for a few minutes, and then I heard her sniff.

"What smells like shit?" She asked.

After that traumatic weekend in the woods, my mom let me quit the Girl Scouts for good, and never volunteered to do anything else group-oriented with me ever again. Maybe she realized that weekend she and I were different; I didn't like the things she liked, you know, like being outdoors, in the woods, and she was okay with that. We never spoke of the retreat in the woods ever again which is probably the best for me. I never found out what bit me, but I learned a valuable lesson that weekend—how to swallow pills when being yelled at by your mother.

The next year I was turning 13, I was finally going to be a teenager, which meant another Team Meeting at St. Louis Children's Hospital. I would have "team meetings" with my doctors (speech, hearing, ENT, plastic surgeon, etc.) to go over my progress and to see if, and when, my next surgery would be scheduled.

The Team Meetings were an entire day of being poked and prodded. The worst part was meeting with the ENT because that usually meant the camera scope down my nose and into my throat to see my pallet.

"Looks like she's going to need braces." Said my dentist who I also met with that day.

Great, so not only was I chubby and awkward, but I was also going to have braces on my teeth. My teen years were about to be uneventful.

The best part was seeing Dr. Marsh, my plastic surgeon, because he was the last person I'd meet with and he would always take my picture to show me my progress.

"Well, it looks like she's ready for her next surgery." He said as he reviewed the notes from the other physicians.

"Which would be?" Asked my parents.

"It's time to build up the cartilage in the palate, so we will take some from the back of her ear to reconstruct the palate. It looks like her speech patterns are doing well, so the speech therapy is helping, but this surgery will help as well." "Looks like we can schedule this as soon as possible." He said as he left the room.

Great, another summer ruined. My parents always scheduled my major surgeries during my summer break so I could heal in time for the next school year and not miss anything. But that also meant that I would be having surgery near my birthday.

That year we had also moved to Florida, so thankfully, I didn't have that many friends that I would miss hanging out with over the summer, but surgery meant that I wasn't able to do much like go swimming in our brand new pool. My summer was going to blow, but I had no idea how much.

# Chapter 2: Ticket to Heaven

I had my fair share of surgeries by the time I was thirteen; I knew the drill. The first step was going to my pediatrician to get the pre-op bloodwork completed to make sure I was healthy enough for anesthesia. The second step typically involved my parents cussing out an insurance company representative for dragging their feet upon approving my surgical procedure. Finally, the third step was flying to my grandma's house where I would stay post-op to recuperate.

I hated surgery day; my mom would wake me up at 3 am so we could make the two-hour drive up to St. Louis for check-in at the hospital. I wasn't allowed to eat past midnight so that meant no breakfast, so not only was I tired, but I was also starving. I also didn't know at the time, but I suffered from huge anxiety, but the Youngs dealt with that just like everything else, just keep it inside. My mom used to call it "growing pains" which wasn't too far off.

When you walk into the entrance of Children's Hospital in St. Louis there is a gigantic ball machine that someone built. I hated that machine for many reasons, but the main reason being the fact that it could just stay there in the lobby pushing its little ball through the mechanical maze so fun and carefree, while I had to have something so incredibly painful done to me. I dreaded hearing that ball in the machine moved around, it just meant my surgery was imminent.

A lot of my anxiety with surgery revolved around the anesthesia part. Since birth, I had experienced the feeling of the loss of control when being put under for surgery. For anyone, anesthesia can be terrifying, but to a child who does not understand the concept, it can be crippling.

"Sit over here while I fill out your paperwork", my mom said as she took the clipboard from the registrar and pointed over to an empty chair.

I took a seat and started playing on my Gameboy when I felt a light tap on my shoulder.

"Hi, I'm Shelly. Are you having surgery today too?"

It was a girl who looked my age hovering above me.

"Yes, unfortunately," I said as I looked down at my game.

"I am having a palate surgery—the doctor is going to take a bone from my hip and put it in my lip." She said as she giggled and continued, "I made that rhyme!"

I looked over to see my mom still talking to the registrar, hoping she would come over to save me from talking to this strange girl.

Okay, so I know that sounds mean, but, oddly enough, I had never really met another cleft lip/palate patient before, and my parents and I never talked about my deformity unless the surgery was coming up, so seeing this girl was like looking into the mirror, and for some reason, I couldn't relate.

"What's your name?" She asked.

"Lindsay," I replied still staring at the Gameboy screen.

"Is that the new Tiny Toon Adventures game?" She asked excitedly.

"Yep," I said as I sighed, knowing this girl wasn't going to go away.

My anxiety was already through the roof and I didn't feel like talking to anyone, especially to her.

"I love that game! Look what I brought with me. The doctor said I'm allowed to bring something from home into my surgery; they told me I couldn't bring my dog, so I guess this is the next best thing." She said as she pulled out a stuffed animal.

"This is Bubba. He talks." She said as she put a stuffed bear on her lap.

Of course, he does.

"Do you want to play with him?" She asked.

I was about to speak when my mom finally walked up to us.

"Oh Lindsay, who is your friend?" She asked.

Shit, she wasn't going to help me out at all.

"Mom this is Shelly, Shelly, this is my mom," I said super enthusiastically.

"Shelly it's so nice to meet you. Are you having surgery today too?" She asked.

Shelly told my mom the same story she told me. She also told her that she lived on a farm in Indiana, which explained a lot.

"You know what I brought my camera to take pictures. Why don't you two get together and I'll take your picture."

"Mom?" I whined.

"Yes really, now behave or you won't get anything from the gift shop." She said as she snapped our picture.

"If you are having surgery first, I'll let you take Bubba with you, so you won't be lonely," Shelly said as she held out her stuffed bear.

"Oh my gosh, that is just the sweetest. Lindsay would love to!" My mom said as she grinned from ear-to-ear.

She was just doing this to piss me off and it was working.

"Lindsay Young?" I heard a voice ask from across the room.

There she was the nurse who was about to take me back to serve my sentence. My mom took my hand and walked me over to meet her.

"Are you ready for your surgery today?" She asked me if I was going to be excited about it.

"Is anyone ever ready for surgery?" I asked her.

My mom gave me a nudge and whispered, "Be nice and respectful."

"Do you have any allergies?" She asked looking at her clipboard.

"She is allergic to Ceclor and Septra. She gets really bad hives and rashes." My mom responded looking over at me.

"Well, Ms. Young, hop on the bed. We're going to take your temperature, get your blood pressure, and pulse. Just to make sure you're going to be safe. Oh, and put in your IV."

My blood pressure shot up as soon as I heard the word IV pour out of her mouth. She said it so lax like it was something as simple as taking a sip of water.

My mind suddenly flashed back to when I was three years old. I was rushed to the hospital in the middle of the night with a severe case of pneumonia; I used to get that a lot, along with ear infections—just another lovely side-effect of having a cleft lip and palate.

This was also coincidentally the same night that Hurricane Hugo decided to hit Charlotte. I was having a lot of trouble breathing because of pneumonia that I needed to have IV antibiotics, but even at that age, I knew what IV's were all about.

Combine the horror of getting an IV and the sound of windows busting out because of the hurricane and you get one terrified little girl. The only thing I could do was fight, and I put up a good one, so much so, that the doctors and nurses had to strap my arms down to put in the IV.

"Mom, why can't they put in the IV after my anesthesia?" I begged.

"You know you have to have one; they have to be able to administer your medicine. How many times have we done this Lindsay? Be a big girl and toughen up." She responded.

Ah, no sympathy there. My mom was very loving and caring, but when it came to things like this—surgeries or being in any kind of pain, she had an immense lack of compassion.

She too had her fair share of trauma growing up as well. When she was thirteen, my age now, she and her sisters (my aunts) were in a serious car accident that left my mom in the hospital for months and in a full-body cast. She knew what pain was, but she also knew that the only way to get through something traumatic was to be strong and power through as she did.

The nurse came back in with a slew of things in her hands, one of which was a prepped needle hooked to a bag. First, she checked my temperature, all fine there, then came the blood pressure cuff that squeezed the life out of my arm. She put her stethoscope up to my pulse point and stated, "Your pulse is really fast, are you nervous?" Me? Nervous? Never.

"She hates IVs." My mom chimed in.

"Oh, it's nothing to be worried about, I will make it so quick that you won't even know it happened." The nurse responded.

Very unlikely, but okay,

"Okay, I want you to close your eyes and think of your favorite place in the whole world." She said as she rubbed smelly alcohol on my arm.

Shit, now there's even more pressure; my favorite place in the whole world? What if I didn't have one? What if I've never been to my favorite place?

"Have you thought of one?" She asked.

"No, I can't think of one," I said scared.

"Have you been to Disney World?" The nurse asked.

My mom immediately looked at the nurse and shook her head "no".

"Unfortunately," I responded.

"Oh no, you didn't like Disney?" The nurse asked.

My mom made the wave of the neck gesture to the nurse to "cut it out".

"No, I didn't. It's not actually the happiest place on Earth. It's a joke." I replied getting extremely irritated at this point.

"Do you like the beach?" She asked.

Eh, it's okay. But just to get her to stop making terrible suggestions I just went with it.

"Uh-huh," I said.

"Close your eyes and imagine you are on a beach right now. The sun is shining on you and the waves are crashing. You are in the sand building a huge castle, can you see it?" She asked.

I shook my head yes.

"Okay, all done." She said with a smile.

What the--? I looked down and there it was, the IV hanging out of my arm, and I didn't feel a thing.

"The anesthesiologist will be right in to speak with you. Lindsay, when you wake up you will be in the recovery room, your mom will be waiting for you. This will be an outpatient procedure so you will get to go home as soon as you wake up. Good luck with your surgery."

We waited and waited for what seemed like forever and finally, the anesthesiologist showed up.

"You ready?" He asked. "Mom, say goodbye, I'm going to wheel her into the OR now."

What the hell? This didn't seem normal—usually, the anesthesiologist would sit down, ask me a couple of questions, and then take me back. I wasn't prepared for this.

"I love you, Lindsay, be brave. I will be right here when you wake up." Said my mom as she kissed me on the forehead.

Then he began to push me through hallways and corridors until we finally made it to the operating room. The anesthesiologist would typically talk to me on our journey, but not today.

There were a few nurses already in the room prepping when I rolled in. They lifted me onto the cold and hard surgery table.

"Long night huh doctor?" I heard one of the nurses ask my anesthesiologist.

"Yeah, I think I celebrated my promotion a little too much, but I'm good." He said.

"Okay, so you know the drill. Once I put the mask on, I want you to count backward from 100, can you do that?" He asked me.

I nodded yes, but I was getting extremely nervous. Once the mask went over my face, my head goes fuzzy, and I lose all control.

"Do we need to restrain her?" I heard one of the nurses ask.

"No, I don't think so." He said.

Ha, you probably should have.

I was lying on my back and all I could see was this huge light glaring in my eyes when all of a sudden, the gas mask popped into my line of sight. The doctor put it over my mouth and told me to breathe.

"I hope you like bubblegum flavor." Said one of the nurses.

"Okay, now count backward from 100." He said.

I could feel my head get fuzzy and my fight or flight senses kicked in and began flailing my arms around.

Everyone in the room gathered around to hold me down as the anesthesiologist kept telling me to breathe, and that was the last thing I remembered hearing.

My eyes slowly opened and I could hear Dr. Marsh and the others talking. Everything was so fuzzy and I couldn't make out what they were saying until I heard a nurse yell.

"Oh my god, she's awake. She's not supposed to be awake. Her eyes are open!"

Then everything turned black.

When I woke up again, I was alone in the room, which was extremely bright. I wasn't hooked up to any machines and it didn't seem like I had anything surgical done to me. I slid off

the surgical table and walked through the OR doors in my hospital gown.

"Mom?" I asked searching for my mom, but there was no one around.

I saw another OR room with the door propped open, so I peeked inside to see if anyone was in there.

"Oh hello." I heard a voice say as soon as I entered the room.

It was a man, an older man with long white hair and a beard. Any kid would have thought it was Santa Claus, but thanks to Lauren Gordon, an old friend, I no longer believed in him.

"Come up here and sit by me." He said sitting on a surgical table.

Now, I know it sounds creepy to have an old man ask a young girl to sit next to him, but there was something about him that seemed unalarming and kind.

I jumped up on the table to sit beside him.

"Lindsay, you have been chosen for this journey, you know that?" He asked.

I assumed he was talking about having a cleft lip and palate, so I went with it and shook my head yes.

"I only pick the strongest people for the hardest challenges. But you know you're not supposed to be here right now, don't you?" he asked me.

I don't even know where I was, so how was I supposed to know?

"You need to go back. Your mother needs you." He said.

Strangely, I wanted to stay there with the weird old man. Something about him, a glow, a feeling of pure love and warmth that I wanted to cling onto.

"She does? Can't I stay just a little bit longer?" I asked.

"No, but I will see you again. Now go back through those doors; your mom is waiting." He said as he pointed at the bright light beaming through the room doors. I hopped off the table and looked back, "Bye" I said.

"Lindsay? Can you hear me?" I heard a voice in the distance getting louder.

"Lindsay, are you awake?" It was my mom's voice.

I nodded yes.

"You're awake!" I heard her yell.

I could hear her, but I couldn't open my eyes.

"Mom, I can't see!" I yelled.

Everything was black and no matter how hard I tried, I couldn't open my eyes.

"What's wrong with your eyes? What's wrong with her eyes?" She asked someone else in the room.

"Let me go get the doctor" I heard a voice say.

"Mom, what happened?" I asked.

"I don't know, but we're sure as hell going to find out." She said angrily.

I heard someone enter the room.

"I see someone's awake." I heard the voice say, it was Dr. Marsh.

"Well, I'm glad that you can see because my daughter fucking can't". She yelled.

He walked up to me and I could feel him open my eyelids.

"Lindsay, can you see this?" He asked.

"I can see a little bit of light," I responded.

"I will call in Dr. Huber, our team ophthalmologist to run some tests and see what is going on." He said.

"Good because I would like to know what the hell is going on with my daughter. She has been in a coma for three damn days and now she can't see. Someone better give me some answers and quick too. You don't want me to make a scene!" She started yelling.

"We are right on it Mrs. Young, we'll find out what's going on." He said.

"Mom, was I really in a coma for three days?" I asked.

"When they wheeled you into recovery, you never woke up. What did they do to you?" She asked.

The next couple of days were nothing but a marathon of tests on my eyes to figure out what happened.

"It looks like she has cornea abrasions on both of her eyes." Said the ophthalmologist.

"And how in the hell would have that happened?" She asked.

"Well, normally, a patient's eyes are taped once they are under anesthesia to prevent this from happening." He responded.

"So, you're telling me that her eyes were not taped?" She asked.

"It appears not." He said.

I was very glad that I was unable to see the fury in my mother's eyes when he told her that bit of news.

"I am going to rip all of their goddamn throats out. What do we do? Will she ever be able to see again?" She yelled.

"We're going to try an antibiotic drop and a steroid drop to help with the inflammation. Those should help her see."

As soon as he put the drops in my eyes, I could see little more bits of light enter through, which was really painful.

"I can see!" I said excitedly.

"Thank God." My mom said.

"Keep her out of direct sunlight for a few days to let her eyes heal." Said the doctor.

The nurse wheeled me back into my room as my mom helped me get back onto my bed.

"Mommala, can I tell you something?" I asked her.

"What is it?" She asked.

"There was something different about this surgery," I said.

"What do you mean?"

"Well, I think I woke up during it," I responded. Even though I couldn't see much; I'm pretty sure my mom's face was turning red with anger.

"You THINK you woke up?" She asked furiously.

I told her what I heard and saw.

"But that's not it. I think I died." I said.


If anyone has seen the movie Terms of Endearment, then you are familiar with the scene where Shirley McLain goes off the rails on the nurse staff for not giving her daughter her pain medicine, well, that doesn't hold a candle to what my mom did to the staff at Children's Hospital.

"I need answers and I need answers NOW or else I will sue every one of you mother fuckers and leave you penniless and begging for food out on the streets of East St. Louis!"

I could hear her yelling from my hospital room. I knew that tone all too well, one I never wanted to hear because as soon as I did, I knew my life was over.

"Mrs. Young, please calm down." Dr. Marsh said as he grabbed her shoulders.

"Calm down? You want me to calm down? You put my daughter in a coma, made her blind, and now, she's telling me she saw God on the operating room table. So, I need answers and I need them NOW!" She yelled.

I bet you could hear her past the Mississippi River. As tiny as she was, you did not want to make my mom angry because she turned into the She-Hulk in a heartbeat.

No one could tell us what happened during my surgery, but it was bad enough that Dr. Marsh and St. Louis Children's Hospital took care of our expenses for that surgery.

My parents never sought out legal ramifications, but that was because Dr. Marsh was the best craniofacial plastic surgeon in the country, and unfortunately, performed his surgeries at St. Louis Children's Hospital. If they had tried to sue him, they would have been in court for years, bleeding out money, and I would have lost the best plastic surgeon in the country.

Word on the street said that my anesthesiologist had partied a little too hard the night before my procedure and wasn't a hundred percent. So much so, that he gave me too little anesthesia that I woke up, and when I did, I scratched my corneas. He freaked out when he saw that I had awakened that he doubled-up on the anesthesia. I had enough anesthesia in my system to knock-out two grown men. Hence the white light and the Santa Claus looking Jesus.

"Well, you did it, Lindsay, you finally did it." Said my mom in the hospital room.

"What? What did I do?" I asked.

"You finally got your death wish." She said.

"Okay Ms. Young, it's time to move you to your new room." A nurse said as she brought in a wheelchair.

"New room?" I asked.

"Now that you can see again, you no longer get special treatment and have to share a room." My mom said as she helped wheel me down to my new room.

Share a room? Seriously?

"Well, here you go Lindsay. Meet your new roomie." My mom said as she pushed me into the room.

"Hey, roomie!"

I looked up and it was Shelly.

Just. Fucking.Great.

# Chapter 3: Wonderwall

I spent most of my recovery at my grandma's house because she lived the closest to the hospital, but I didn't get much rest while I was there. Word got out that my mom and I were "visiting", so our entire extended family decided to pop by and check out the sideshow freak with the huge bandage around her head, which my mom tried to make light of and tell me that Madonna had one just like it. Yeah okay, like that was true.

 Dr. Marsh took cartilage from behind my ear to mold more of my palate and touched up my lip, which left me with the ugliest head dressing and a huge scar on my mouth. My grandma made the best food while the company was over, but of course, I couldn't eat any of it due to the stitches in my mouth.

It was summer and I couldn't go out and play with my brother or my cousins; I was stuck inside with an old lady and in my feels.

But I never let the pain bother me or stop me from doing what I wanted. The doctors always said I was the only patient who was discharged earlier than any other patient. Well that's because I hated hospitals and I had shit to do—I wasn't going to let a major surgery stop me. Even though my determination didn't help me much when it came to recovery because my mom and my grandma were like the Nazi Gestapo when it came to deter me from going outside to play with my cousins. Understandably so, my family tried to kill each other any chance they got, so my mom couldn't risk it.

Finally, after a month of isolation, I had my post-op check-up at the hospital and was permitted to fly on the plane back home to Florida, hallelujah!

"Ma'am, are you sure she's safe to fly?" Asked an airline ticket associate.

"Of course! I pumped her full of pain meds so she can't feel a thing". My mom responded pointing over at me looking annoyed in a wheelchair.

As if it weren't enough to have a huge beehive bandage over my head, I also had to be wheeled in a chair to the gate like an invalid. Why couldn't I have just stayed dead and avoid the embarrassment?

"Mom can I just walk?" I begged.

"No, we will get on the plane first because you are special needs." She said.

"Oh my god, I am not special needs!" I yelled.

A TWA flight attendant walked up to us in the middle of our argument.

"Excuse me, I couldn't help but overhear. My niece is also special needs and I just want to let you know that I am here to help you any way I can." She said to my mom.

"Aw, that is so kind of you." My mom responded.

"I am not special needs so can you please fuck off?" I told the flight attendant.

My mom looked over at the woman and said, "She has Turrets".

Obviously, I didn't have any of those things, but my mom did give me a double dose of pain meds so I would pass out on the airplane, but pain meds also made me very mean and very bitchy.

We finally made it home and was greeted by my dad at the gate (yes, this was pre-9/11 so we could still do cool shit like that). My dad didn't typically come to my surgeries which didn't bother me much because I knew he had to work to pay for them. I was so happy to see him and so happy to finally be home.

My room was my oasis; it was every 90s teenager's dream room equipped with a blacklight, a 5 CD changer with a karaoke feature, and walls filled with N*SYNC pictures. I was convinced that Justin Timberlake was going to see me at a show or in the mall, pluck me from obscurity, and make me his girlfriend—it's all written in a letter I sent to him, but he had yet to reply.

I had a month and a half left until I started in my new school and I was going to make the most of it.

It was my birthday; I was finally thirteen, and official a teenager (whatever that meant). Usually, I would have had a huge party to celebrate, but since I was still recovering and we had just moved; I didn't have that many friends—okay, I didn't have any friends. And so, it was a small celebration with my family which typically involved dinner at my favorite restaurant followed by presents and cookie cake at the house.

I made a wish and blew out the candle; my brother got me an import N*SYNC CD that I didn't have, and my parents bought me a new pair of rollerblades.

"You can't use these until your face is finally healed. Even then, I'm not sure if you should. What if you fall and mess something up?" My mom said as she picked up the reminisce of wrapping paper.

"Well, why did you even buy these if you don't want me to use them?" I asked justifiably.

"You need to be more active, especially before school starts." She replied taking the plate of cake away from me. That was her kind way of saying I should lose weight. "You know how kids can be, especially at a new school. Which by the way, we are meeting with the pastor next week."

Ah yes, my brother and I would be attending a private Christian school, which was new for us. We had always gone to public school, but because Florida, is, well, Florida—my parents thought we would get a better education and stay out of trouble in a private school.

"Should I bring my bible?" I asked.

"Don't be a smartass Lindsay; honestly, you need a little Jesus." My mom smirked.

"No I don't; I met Jesus and he said I am doing just fine," I said as I grabbed my new skates and went to my room.

The next day my mom went running errands while my brother was off doing god knows what, so I decided to take my new rollerblades on a test drive.

I strapped myself in and off I went down my neighborhood street. I knew how to skate on roller skates; I learned after I saw Oksana Baiul win the gold medal at the 1994 Winter Olympics—somehow, I thought roller skating and figure skating were the same things. Plus, I spent a lot of my elementary school days at the local roller rink watching the couples in envy slow skating to K-Ci and Jojo, hoping that someday I would do that with someone.

I decided to skate a little further down to the next street—wow, I'm really good at this, I thought to myself as I turned the corner. Then all of a sudden, I felt something, or someone hit me and I fell to the ground. So, before you ask, no, I wasn't wearing a helmet—it was the '90s and nobody wore a helmet unless you were a loser or an idiot like me.

This has to be it; this has to be how I die.

I could see the bright light, the same bright light I saw during my surgery, as I slowly opened my eyes. I could see a blurry figure hovering above me; could it be my Santa looking friend? It took a moment for my eyes to focus because the light was so bright.

"Holy shit, are you okay?" I heard a voice ask. It was a woman.

I opened my eyes more and she started to become into focus.

"Can you move?" She asked.

"Uh, I think so. What happened?" I asked as I began to sit up.

"Whoa whoa, slowly," She said as she helped me sit up.

"Did you hit me with your car?" I asked her.

"No, I was just walking, but some asshole hit you and drove off."

"Great," I said as I began to inspect my body.

"Are you sure you are okay? Maybe we can call someone?" She asked.

"No, no. I can move everything. I live just down the street." I said.

"Well here, let me help you. Your knees look pretty scraped up and your blades are toast." She said pointing down to my newly damaged rollerblades.

"Shit, my parents are going to kill me," I said as I slowly stood up.

She grabbed my arm and helped me get stable.

"Maybe you should take those off to walk," She said.

"Thanks for your help, but I think I've got this.," I said as I unbuckled my blades.

"I'll walk with you, make sure your safe and all." She said with a smile.

"Listen, lady, that is nice of you, but I don't know who you are, and being as I have already been a victim of a kidnapping, I don't want to double my odds."

"You can trust me." She said.

"Isn't that what people say when they are untrustworthy?"

"Oh c'mon, I'm harmless." She replied.

"That is also what psychos say right before they kill someone," I said as I began to walk away from her.

"Let me walk you to your street just so I can make sure you're okay." She insisted.

"Fine, but that is as far as you go," I said trying to set boundaries with this lady.

She looked young, but I couldn't tell what age she was, but she was really pretty.

We began to walk back to my street when she began to ask me questions.

"So, do you have a death wish or something?"

I looked at her with my eyebrows raised as if it was the weirdest question to ask.

"No. It just seems to follow me everywhere I go." I responded.

"Lindsay's got nine lives." She said.

"How do you know my name?" I asked her freaked out.

"You told me."

"No, I'm pretty sure you didn't," I said defensively.

"Yes, you did. It was one of the questions I asked you to make sure you were okay." She replied.

I'm pretty sure I didn't but I was tired of this woman already and I couldn't wait to ditch her.

"Ok, this is my street. Thanks for, well, I guess walking with me." I said as I turned around.

"I'm sure we'll see each other again soon." She yelled.

That is so creepy, who says that? God, I hoped I'd never see her again.

The following day I was at the local grocery store helping my mom who was busy chatting with another mom she met in our neighborhood when I hear a voice from behind me.

"See I told you we'd see each other again."

Oh fuck, it was her, the creepy lady.

"Are you following me or something because my dad is in law enforcement (lie) and he will come after you so fast," I tried to whisper so my mom wouldn't overhear me.

She laughed and said, "Follow you? You must be following me. I just came to get limes for my margaritas. That's your mom, huh?" She asked.

"Oh my god, what is wrong with you. Can you please just leave me alone and stop following me?" I begged.

She shrugged her shoulders and sighed.

"Okay, so I guess I haven't been honest with you about who I am." She said.

"Oh my god, is this one of those Oprah moments where you tell me that my dad has an entirely different family, and you are my half-sister or some shit?" I asked.

She laughed.

"Not hardly. Are you sure you want me to explain this now? With your mom right there?" She asked.

"Um, now is as good of a time as any," I said annoyed.

"Promise you won't freak out?" She asked.

"Oh my god just tell me already!" I said under my breath.

"Okay, and please don't think I'm crazy."

"Hm too late for that," I said.

"Okay, here it goes—I am your, well, I guess you can call me your—gosh, this is a lot harder to put into words than I thought."

"Just fucking say it!" I yelled.

"I am your life guide." She responded as she looked confused about what she had just said.

"Life guide? What is that like a fairy godmother?" I said almost laughing.

"Ew, that makes me sound super old and it's not PC to say godmother where I'm from because, well, gender roles are super tricky and a sensitive issue." She kept spouting off.

"Where are you from?" I asked, not even sure why I was even entertaining this lunatic.

She smiled like she was proud, "Well, I guess you could say that I am from the future, but all time is fluid so that's just easier to say, but it's really hard to explain."

I started laughing. "Oh my god, you are crazy, like totally batshit crazy. Please leave me alone or I will have my dad on your ass so fast."

"See the thing is, I can't leave you until my "job" is done." She said.

"What's your job? Are you going to kill me?" I asked freaked out.

"For the last time, I was not sent to kill you, I mean, at least I don't think so. It was kind of vague on what I was supposed to do with you except give you some advice and steer you in the right direction." She said confused.

"Who sent you? The aliens? Santa Claus? God?"

"I can't tell you that, sorry. I also can't tell you anything about your future—it was specifically stated in my contract."

"Linz, are you ready to go?" I heard my mom shout from the end of the aisle. Thank god.

"Listen, if you follow me or contact me again…"

"When you were five, you and your brother got in trouble for shoving Wizard of Oz toys down the toilet." She said.

"How do you know that?" I asked shocked. No one but my family knew about that.

"Linz, c'mon, I'm leaving." My mom yelled.

"There is a park and a lake behind my neighborhood. I will meet you there tomorrow at 3 pm." I said.

"I will be there," She said as she gave me a wave as I walked off.

"Who the hell were you talking to?" My mom asked.

"Did you see her?" I asked my mom.

"See who? You were whispering to yourself in the aisle. Am I going to have to call a shrink? Dear god."

My mouth fell to the floor. Was I going crazy? I had to find out if I was the only person who could see this woman because if so, then I was the crazy one.

All I could think about was the fact that I was probably losing my mind and all of these questions came flooding in my mind.

So, what if I died during surgery and I was living in purgatory? Or what if this woman was just a figment of my imagination made up to cope with a traumatic experience.

My mind was going in so many directions and I couldn't wait to get some answers.

The next day felt like an eternity, which it probably was if I was dead, but it was finally almost 3 pm so I made my way to the lake.

I found an empty bench right by the water and out in the open just in case this woman was crazy and tried to snatch me. I was watching the ducks swim around in the lake when I felt someone sit down next to me—finally, some answers.

I look over and it was a boy, he looked like he was my age, maybe a little bit older.

"Excuse me, this seat is taken," I said kind of rudely.

He smiled, "I don't see anyone sitting here at the moment."

"Well, she's not here yet, but when she does get here that is where she is going to sit," I replied.

He laughed under his breath, "Well then, I guess I'll just have to keep it warm for her."

"It's like 100 degrees outside," I said getting kind of nervous.

"It's a figure of speech. I'm Billy by the way." He said as he reached his hand out for me to shake. Who does that?

"Hi, Billy By the Way," I said as I put my hands under my legs and looked in a different direction trying to avoid conversation.

"And what might your name be?" He asked as he bent forward trying to get me to look at him.

"Lindsay, my name is Lindsay. Why are you sitting here?" I asked abruptly.

"Well, Lindsay, nice to meet you. You must be new here because I've never seen you in the neighborhood before and you don't go to my school, but because you asked so nicely, I'm sitting here because this is my usual seat. You're sitting on my bench."

"I don't see your name on it," I said sarcastically.

"You don't? Look a little harder next to you." He said smiling from ear-to-ear.

I looked down and there it was etched into the wood, the name "Billy".

I just looked up at him and didn't say anything.

"I come here pretty much every day to feed the ducks. They all have names you know?" He asked.

"Let me guess, Hughie, Louis, and Dewey?"

"C'mon, give me a little credit, I am much more original than that. See that one with the white tail? That is Oscar. The one next to him is Charles, and the one behind them is Frost."

"Frost?" I asked.

"Well, William Frost, but William is also my name, so I didn't want anyone to get confused. See, I named them all after—"

"Authors." I interrupted.

"Very good. Do you like any of them?" He asked.

"Who? The ducks or the authors?" I joked.

He laughed, "You're really funny Lindsay. Will I be seeing you in English class?"

"Depends. Which school do you go to?" I asked.

"I will be attending Ridgedale High this year—9th grade."

"Oh, I will be Alfer's Christian Academy—8th grade," I said.

"Ah, private school. Very lucky; your parents must really care about you." He said.

What a weird thing to say.

"Why do you say that?" I asked.

"Oh, well, I'm sure you know that public schools here are not the best, so your parents must care enough to want to send you to a good school."

"Yeah, they're cool. Listen, it was nice chatting with you, but it looks like my friend isn't going to show, so I've got to go." I said as I stood up and started to walk away.

"I could walk with you?" He asked.

What is it with these people wanting to walk with me so badly?

"No, it's cool. I'm sure your ducks would like some one-on-one time with you."

Ugh, why did I say that?

"Maybe I'll see you around?" He shouted.

I whispered, "Unlikely", and shouted, "Okay!"


What the hell? She didn't show up. Maybe she didn't exist, and it was a one-time thing, well, two-time thing. I just shrugged it off and went back home to help with dinner.

"Linz, take a shower before bed. We have to be up early to meet with the Pastor at your new school tomorrow morning." My mom said as she washed the dishes from dinner.

I took and shower and I couldn't stop thinking about how weird things have been ever since my surgery. I guess it didn't help that there were a lot of new things that happened like the move to Florida and now starting a new school year at a new school; that was just added pressure. Maybe everything was just all in my head.

My mom, brother, and I woke up at the crack of dawn and headed over to Alfers, my new school. The school was not impressive; it was a chapel where services were held and two smaller attached buildings. The first building was for the daycare and pre-k through 5th graders. The second building was ours; 6th grade through 12th grade.

There was only a maximum of 15 students per classroom, so we were going to get to know our new classmates very well.

We ended the tour in the chapel where my mom and the pastor discussed tuition (which was astronomical considering what they were paying for) while my brother toured the building. I decided to sit down in a pew and wait for my mom gazing at the giant Jesus statue hanging above the baptizing pool.

"Do you think that's what he really looks like?"

"Holy fuck!" I yelled.

It was her, the stranger. She just appeared right next to me.

She laughed and said, "Shhhh, you really shouldn't say stuff like that in the house of the lord."

"Why are you here? You were supposed to meet with me yesterday at the lake. Where were you?" I asked furiously.

"I saw you there talking to that cute boy and I didn't want to interrupt."

"I really needed to talk to you, you could have walked up we weren't talking about anything important, and he's not cute."

She smirked, "Okay, I'm sorry. What do you want to talk about?" She asked.

"Um, for starters, how can you just pop in and out like this? And why am I the only one who can see you? Am I dead?" I kept asking.

"You are not dead. I am here and here for you only, no one else can see me but you, and I come whenever you need me. Like I said in the grocery store, I can't disclose everything to you, but I am here until you don't need me anymore. I am your life guide— a counselor."

"Who sent you?" I couldn't believe I had to ask a question like that.

She got silent.

“Tell me,” I said frustrated.

“You did, you sent me.”

# Chapter 4: Rollin' With My Homies

Did I send her? How could I have sent her? I was so confused, but at the same time just frustrated enough that I decided to go with it. If I needed this weirdo woman to help me with my messed-up life, then sure, why not let her help me?

"Fine, whatever. Since I am the only one who can see you, can you please stop popping up out of nowhere? My parents really will think I'm insane and send me off to a mental institution."

"Got it!" She said as she held out her hand for me to shake on it, which I did, reluctantly.

I looked over and my mom was now talking to a woman I've never seen before. Another thing you should know about my mom is that she never met a stranger; she could talk to anyone for hours and never get tired. I was quite the opposite; never spoke unless spoken to and pretty much kept to myself. I tried to avoid being seen at all costs, probably to spare the questions about what was going on with my face or to avoid the ridicule—it worked so far.

I saw my mom waving me to come over to her.

"Great, I've got to go," I said I stood up.

"I guess I'll be seeing you around." Said my weird imaginary guide.

"Oh, do you have a name?" I asked her.

She smiled, "Not really, but you can call me P."

I laughed out loud.

"P? Like I have to go pee or the initial P?" I asked still laughing.

"Haha, you're so funny. Like the initial P." She said.

"That is so weird, but again, you are weird so I wouldn't expect anything less," I said as I walked away.

"Oh, just say yes!" P yelled.

"Say yes? To what?" I tried to whisper so my mom wouldn't hear me.

P smiled and said, "Oh, you'll find out!"

I hated this vague bullshit.

I walked up to my mom and her new best friend.

"Lindsay this is Shirley, Shirley's kids go here too. Her daughter is a year younger than you and will be going into 7th grade, isn't that great?"

I could tell my mom was using her "fake" voice. The voice she would only use around other people who were not her family.

"Wow mom, that really is great!" I said using my "fake" voice.

She gave me the side-eye and I knew I had to behave.

"Where's your brother?" Asked my mom to me.

"I don't know, I'm not his keeper," I said.

"Hi mom, I'm up here!" He said waving to us from the pool they use to Baptize people.

"Jesus Christ!" My mom said as she ran to get him down.

"It'll be my daughter's first year here too," Shirley said to me.

"Did she go to public school?" I asked her.

"No, she and her brother Zach went to a different private school near here and they didn't like it very much, so we are going to give Alfers a try."

"Yeah me too," I said as I saw my mom as she dragged my brother.

"I apologize Shirley, but I've got to get these two demon spawns home before they burn the chapel down." My mom said as she scrambled to find her keys.

"Me too, there is no telling what my kids have done to the house while I was gone," Shirley said laughing.

"I've seen you guys around the neighborhood." My brother said to Shirley.

"You live in Hunter Ridge too?" Shirley asked.

"We do!" My mom said excitedly.

I looked at her like she was insane; she never got that excited about anything, well, except making my life a living hell.

"Yay! Now I have a wine buddy! And hey Lindsay, you and Maggie should meet sometime. She could really use a friend." Said Shirley.

Did I miss something? Who the hell was Maggie? Oh wait, her daughter. Got it.

"Yeah, that would be cool," I said trying not to sound too excited about it.

The last thing I needed starting a new school was to have a younger hanger-on. I had to make a good first impression, otherwise, I will be the freak of the school, and that spot was already reserved for my brother.

The next day I was getting ready to head out on my bike when I was stopped by my mom.

"Where do you think you're going?" She asked.

"Riding around the neighborhood; Daniel and a couple of his friends want to ride up to the convenient store," I said as I grabbed an apple for the road.

"Oh no, you're not. You are hanging out with Maggie today." She said as she took the apple from my hands.

"What? I don't want to hang out with her. She's younger than me; I need friends my own age and not some baby."

"The only one who is being a baby is you. Plus, she is only a year younger than you, and I already told Shirley you would spend the day with her. Maggie is really excited to meet you, so could you be nice? I know it's really hard for you, but could you at least try?" She asked.

"Ugh, fine," I said as I started to storm off.

"Oh, and I told her you guys could go roller-skating; you can try out the new skates we got you for your birthday." She yelled.

Fuck.

I heard the doorbell ring, and it was Shirley and Maggie.

"Hi Lindsay, this is Maggie, Maggie this is Lindsay," Shirley said introducing us.

"Hi," I said unenthusiastically.

"Hi! It's so nice to meet you!" She said as she ran up and hugged me.

Hella awkward since I wasn't the touchy, feely kind at all.

"Well, I'll leave you two to have fun. Maggie, just be home by 5 pm okay?" Shirley said as she walked away.

"Okay, mom!" Maggie replied with a wave goodbye.

"So, what do you like to do for fun?" I asked Maggie.

"Oh, just about anything. My mom said that we could roller skate today if you'd like?" She asked me.

"You see, I would love to, but my skates are out of commission right now." Referring to the fact that I utterly wrecked them when I got hit.

"Well, that's okay, I have an extra pair you can use." She said excitedly.

Great.

"Do you want to meet up with my brother and his friends at the lake? I think they are headed to the gas station up the road." I said to Maggie as I laced up my borrowed skates.

"Sure, you don't think that's too far to go on skates?" She asked.

"Nah, I do it all the time," I told her, totally lying. I wasn't sure I could do it, but I wasn't going to let her know that and risk looking cool.

"Awesome! You ready?" She asked me.

"Yep!" I said as I stood up. Maggie looked at my scraped knees.

"Ouch, how did that happen?" She asked.

"Oh, that? That's nothing, just took a tumble trying new tricks on the bike." I said as I lied to her a second time.

"Oh wow, you are really cool Lindsay." She said in awe of me.

I had a little fan which I wasn't used to.

We started to skate towards the lake, and I was doing well, but I already knew that it was going to be a struggle by the way I was heavy breathing.

"Do you want to stop and take a break?" Asked Maggie who was skating with ease.

"Nope, I'm good," I said as I hustled faster.

We finally made it to the lake; I could see my brother on his bike talking to a couple of his friends, so Maggie and I skated up to them.

"What are you doing here you little punk?" I heard one of the boys say.

"We wanted to see what you guys were up to," Maggie said to the boy who just spoke.

He was the most beautiful creature I had ever seen. He was tall and slender, but with a little bit of muscle on him. His hair was dark brown and cut like Jonathan Taylor Thomas, with the bluest eyes that even oceans would be jealous of, and a smile unlike any other I had seen before. I never believed in love at first sight until that moment.

"Aren't you going to introduce me to your friend?" He asked Maggie.

Wait, they knew each other?

"Lindsay this is Zach, my brother. Zach this is my new friend Lindsay." She said.

"Lindsay it is a pleasure to meet you. Wait, Lindsay, are you two brother and sister?" He asked my brother.

"Yep, this is my little sister." My brother replied.

"That is hilarious. We're all friends." Zach said as he flashed that huge, gorgeous, thousand-watt smile of his.

"Well, I'm Bobby. Bobby Brown. And no, not like the singer. I am the white Bobby Brown." Said the other boy standing there.

"Hi, Bobby, nice to meet you," I said as I tried to hide the fact that I was breathing so hard from the trek to the lake.

"You guys want to go with us to the convenient store to get snacks?" Zack asked looking directly at me.

"Yeah, sure. I mean, that would be dope." I said trying to sound cool.

He laughed.

"Bro, your sister is a trip." He said as he hopped on his bike looking like a straight-up dreamboat.

"You guys can follow us!" Zach said as he waved us on.

Ok, pep talk time. I had to muster up all of the strength I had to skate a mile down the road to the store. I could do it, I had to, I couldn't look like a dork with no stamina in front of the gorgeous hottie bestowed upon me. I had to look cool, effortless, athletic—pretty much everything I wasn't.

"How are you doing Lindsay? Let me know if you need to break okay?" Maggie said trying to sound supportive.

"Oh, I'm good. Easy breezy!" I said lying to her a third time.

My legs felt like Jell-O and I couldn't feel my legs at all which made it easier to push myself harder, but my breathing was becoming a problem.

Having a cleft palate came with its own set of problems, one of them being prohibited from breathing out of the nostril where the cleft was located. I had learned from an early age that breathing through my nose was nearly impossible, so mouth breathing was where it was at, which wasn't helpful when it came to exercise.

We finally made it to the store, and I was about to die. I was breathing so hard that I wanted to vomit, and then pass out.

"You guys made it!" Zach said as he reached up to give me a high-five.

I had my hands on my knees as I looked up at him.

"You don't look so good, let's sit you down and get you some water." He said as he tried to grab me.

"You're so nice," I said as everything turned black.

My worst nightmare happened; I literally passed out in front of a cute boy.

"Oh my god, wake up. Wake up, you're embarrassing me." I heard a voice say.

It wasn't my brother, or Maggie, or Bobby.

"Get up!"

Wait, I knew that voice. It was P.

I slowly opened my eyes and saw her silhouette standing over me. When I opened my eyes more she faded away and it was Zach.

"Are you okay?" He asked as he helped me up.

"Yeah, I guess I just got a little light-headed. Blood sugar drops am I right?" I said trying to laugh it off.

My brother looked at me like I was so full of shit. He knew.

"Here, drink my water. Let's let her sit here a minute before we head back." Zach said as he whispered in my ear, "You can ride on my bike with me on the way back if that's okay?" He asked. I nodded my head yes as I smiled and took a big drink of water.

I rode on the back of his bike all the way home holding onto his shoulders.

"This was really fun; we should do it again," Zach said looking directly at me. "But you should probably stick to a bike from now on." He said as he winked at me.

"Maggie, I'll see you at home," He said as he rode off on his bike.

"My brother is so weird." She said as we walked into my house.

"You want to go listen to music?" I asked her.

"Yes! I want to see your music collection!" Maggie said with such excitement.

We went to my room and I had a rack full of CDs, all carefully categorized and alphabetized.

"Are you a N*SYNC or Backstreet fan?" I asked her.

"Oh N*SYNC all the way. I think Lance Bass is so cute." She said as she pointed to one of the many posters on my wall.

I knew we would be great friends.

"Which one is your favorite?" She asked.

But before I could answer I heard my mom bust through my door.

"Lindsay! What the hell happened to these?" She yelled as she held up my damaged skates.

I paused so I could think of a good lie to tell her, but before I could speak Maggie started to speak.

"Mrs. Young, Lindsay had a bad fall today. I saw the whole thing; it was like the rock came out of nowhere and there she went. Her knees are a little banged up, but unfortunately, the skates suffered a far worse fate."

"Well, I'm glad you're okay, but you are going to have to explain this to your dad when he comes home." My mom said.

I looked over at Maggie and she gave me a wink.

"Maggie, do you want to stay for dinner?" I asked her.

"We have plenty of food if it's okay with your mom." My mom said as she looked at the skates.

"I would love that. I'll call her right now and tell her." She said.

I knew at that moment that I could trust Maggie, that she was going to have my back no matter what, and who wouldn't want a friend like that?

"Mom, can Maggie spend the night tonight?" I asked.

"Oh, now you want her to spend the night. I think you made a new friend today, huh?" My mom said pestering me.

"Can she?" I asked again.

"I don't know. Your brother just asked if he could have some of his friends over tonight."

"Really? Did he say which ones?" I asked as my eyes lit up.

"No, you know him, you have to pry every little detail out of him. Why don't you go ask him yourself?"

"Well if he has his friends over, I am going to need some back-up. Can she please stay over if her parents say 'Yes'?" I asked for the third time.

"Fine. If her parents agree then that should be fine. I am going to need more wine if that's the case." My mom said as she walked away.

"Maggie, do you want to spend the night?" I asked her.

"Yes! I'll go home and ask my mom right now. I'll call you to let you know what she says."

"Let me know if I need to use my power of persuasion on her," I said with an evil laugh.

Her mom said "Yes", and I was so excited, not only for a sleepover with Maggie, but I was excited that Zach was going to be sleeping over at my house too.

Sleepovers at my house were epic events. I always loved having my friends stay over at my house, but I never liked going over to their homes because most of the time their home life was pretty awkward whereas mine was semi-normal.

My mom made Maggie and me hamburgers, fries, and her famous milkshakes.

"Mom, where is Daniel?" I asked.

"He's at the movies with his friends, they'll be home later."

"Good, we can have girl time!" Maggie said.

We played a couple of rounds of Mall Madness and I won, of course. No one loved shopping more than me and no one could spend money like me either. I guess I should have been nice and let Maggie win at least once, but that just wasn't who I was as a person.

"I have an idea. My mom gave me a bunch of her nightgowns and robes. Do you want to dress up and pretend we are Celine Dion in her "It's All Coming Back to Me Now" video?" I asked her.

"Of course I do!" She said excitedly.

We did our glam and were ready to perform. I was always loved to dress up and perform theatrical versions of songs; Madonna's "Like A Prayer" was my usual go-to song and then eventually anything by Britney Spears.

My mom had her video camera and was ready to film our not-so-well-planned-out performance.

Maggie and I ran throughout the house in our nightgowns pretending we were Celine in the video. I could tell Maggie was having the best time; she loved to laugh, and she was always so happy.

We were laughing so hard that we had to stop.

"Alright, I'll let you girls have your fun. Your brother and his friends should be heading back here soon. I don't want you staying up too late." My mom said as she left us to ourselves.

 "Thank you so much for this. I needed a night like this." Maggie said as we went back to my room.

"Oh yeah, no problem. Did you have friends at your old school?" I asked her.

"Some, but no one as cool as you or your family." She said.

"Well, I'm cool, I don't know about them," I said laughing.

"No, you're all cool. I wish my family were like yours." She said.

"What do you mean?" I asked her; curious to know more, especially about Zach.

"My dad is hardly ever home, but when he is, it's not fun like your family. My dad and my mom are usually fighting." She said.

"Well, you are welcome here any time if you ever need a break from that," I told her. I added, "And thank you for what you did today with my mom."

"No problem, anytime, my friend." She said as she hugged me.

I smiled. I couldn't remember the last time someone called me their "friend." Don't get me wrong, I wasn't a total loser, I had friends, but not a best friend. We never lived in a place long enough for me to have a best friend, and I didn't like people getting too close to me either, but Maggie was different, she was the real deal.

Then, I heard the front door open and my dogs started barking.

I gasped, "The boys are here!"

Maggie laughed, "Do you like anyone?" She asked.

"Like? As in like, like anyone?" I asked her back.

"All of my friends usually end up having a crush on my brother which is so annoying. They don't know how much of a brat he is either." She explained.

"A brat?" I asked.

"Yeah, he thinks he is God's gift to girls and that he can get away with everything, which he usually does, and I can't stand it."

"Well, I don't like your brother," I said lying to her for a fourth time that day.

"Good! See I knew you were different; you can see right through him." She said all giddy.

I pursed my lips and nodded.

"Let's go see what they're up to," I said to her curiously.

"Okay!"

Maggie and I snuck through the house and we could hear the TV on in the living room and a whole bunch of ruckus.

"They are in the front room; let's sneak up on them and scare them," I whispered to Maggie.

She laughed and shook her head "Yes".

"1...2...3..."

As we both yelled, "Boo" at the same time.

"Linz get out of here!" Daniel said as he sat beside Bobby and someone else underneath a blanket.

It had to be Zach!

"Look, you scared him," Bobby said as he patted the body inside the blanket.

Then, he popped out of the blanket and roared like a lion.

 It wasn't Zach.

# Chapter 5: Lovefool

"It's you!", I yelled as I pulled the cover to my nightgown tighter.

It was Billy, the boy that I met at the lake a few days earlier.

"It's you, and what are you wearing?" He asked trying to hold back his laughter.

"None of your business. What are you doing here?" I asked looking over at my brother who was the obvious culprit as to why the strange boy was at our house.

"He's my friend and I invited over." My brother, a person of many words.

"Where's Zach?" I asked, annoyed that he wasn't there, but somehow Billy was invited.

"Oh, my brother had to stay home and help my dad with something—I forgot to tell you." Maggie chimed in.

Lovely, now the one person I wanted to see wasn't there and I had this weird boy staying the night at my house.

"Just don't bother us tonight," I said as I began to walk away.

"Nice to see you again!" Billy yelled as I looked back at him and he gave me a wink.

Ugh, ew. Why was he so weird? And why did my brother befriend him?

Maggie and I stayed up late talking about random things until she passed out. Meanwhile, I was having a hard time trying to fall asleep, and my mouth was dry from all of the talking, so I decided to sneak out and grab a glass of water from the kitchen.

I was trying my best to be as quiet as possible as I opened the cabinet to grab a glass. The glass I wanted was too high for me to reach so I tried to jump to grab it.

"Here, let me get that for you." A voice said as it scared the shit out of me.

I screamed.

"Shhhh, you're going to wake up the whole house."

It was Billy.

"I could kick your ass for that," I said trying to whisper.

"I would like to see you try." He said laughing.

He handed me the glass, "Here you go. Try not to make any more noise. Some people would like to drink their milk in silence."

"Oh, so you just decided to make yourself welcome and treat yourself to our milk, huh?" I asked.

"No one was up to ask, and I was thirsty." He said as he raised his glass as if he were toasting me.

Why was he so annoying?

I grabbed my water and started to walk back to my room.

"Where are you going?" He asked.

"Back to bed which is where you should be too," I said frustrated.

"Here, come sit and talk." He said as he patted the empty barstool next to him.

"I thought you wanted to be in silence?" I asked.

"Well, now that you're here, I'd rather talk to you." He said.

I don't know why, but I decided to sit down.

"So, you like Zach huh?" He asked as I was taking a drink and spit it out.

"What? Who said that?" I asked trying to sound shocked.

"No one, but the way you asked about him tonight just made me put two-and-two together." He turned to me. "He's not the guy you think he is, trust me, I've known him since we were kids."

"Why are you telling me this?" I asked him.

"You seemed like a nice girl, but now I'm not so sure." He said laughing.

"Shhh, keep it down," I whispered. "Plus, you don't know anything about me," I added.

He got quiet for a second.

"I would like to know you. I find you oddly interesting, even though you're mean to me." He said as he took another sip of milk.

"Whatever, no I'm not." I disagreed.

I don't know why I was taking his comments so personally, but I wanted to prove him wrong.

"I suppose we can try to be friends," I said as I rolled my eyes.

"Good to hear, friend." He said with a mile-long grin on his face.

"I'm going to bed," I said as I jumped off the barstool.

"What happened to the nightgown?" He asked as he looked at my pajamas. "I kind of liked it." He added with a wink.

"GO TO BED!" I said as I turned around and a smile came over my face out of nowhere.

After our guests left the next day, my mom wanted to take my brother and me shopping for new school clothes. School clothes shopping was a major event in our household, especially for me because I loved clothes and I loved to shop, but my brother could care less.

We went to the local mall where everyone took their kids shopping in the late '90s. There were parents and kids my age everywhere being dragged from store-to-store to find the perfect outfit.

To me, the mall was my playground, and when I tried on a new outfit, I could be anyone I wanted to be and it didn't matter.

We ended up at one of the biggest department chains in the mall; my brother went off in a different direction as I stuck close to my mom. She took me over to the teen's section, since I just became one a few days earlier, and we browsed a few racks.

Then, I looked up and saw a giant picture of Britney Spears wearing head-to-toe Tommy Hilfiger and I knew I had to look like her. Except, I didn't look like her at all, which I found out quickly when I was in the dressing room trying on the outfit she was wearing in the picture.

I walked out of the dressing room wearing the shorts and shirt that matched Britney's and saw the look on my mom's face.

"No way, your belly is popping out. You can't wear that, take it off and try something else on." She said shaking her head.

"But mom I have to have this outfit, Britney Spears is wearing it." I pleaded.

"I don't care who is wearing it, you're not. Plus, Britney Spears isn't—" and then she stopped.

"Isn't? Isn't what?" I started to yell as tears began to well up in my eyes.

"If you don't keep your voice down, I will pop you right here in front of everyone. And you won't get any new clothes today, how about that?" She said as she got in my face.

I went back into the dressing room and lost it; I was uncontrollably crying.

I had my face in my hands as the tears kept flowing down.

"Now, now, why are you crying?"

It was P.

"Of course, you show up now, I don't need you right now, can you go away, please?" I said sobbing.

"Sorry, no can do. I'm here to help you, remember? So, let me help you. Tell your friend P what happened." She said as she reluctantly put her arm around me.

"It's my mom, she's being a total bitch." I said as I cried harder.

"What did she do?" P asked.

"I really like this outfit and felt really good about it, but when I walked out my mom basically said it was trash and that I looked fat in it."

"I'm sure she didn't say all of that." P said trying to calm me down.

"Were you here? No. If she didn't say it, she implied it."

P got quiet for a second, either distracted by something or trying to figure out the right words to say to me.

"Your mom only has the best intentions, now, she may not sugar coat things like some moms might, but she does love you."

"How do you know? You know nothing about me." I said acting defensively.

"I know a lot about you, okay, but we're not here to talk about that. All I'm saying is, I don't know a lot of moms or parents who care enough about their kids to take them shopping for new clothes, to give their kids a jump start starting the new year off at school on the right foot. Some kids don't have that privilege or parents who have the means to do so."

"Oh, so now you're trying to make me feel bad for the kids who are less fortunate than I am? What good are you?" I said as I stood up.

"I'm just saying that your mom only wants the best for you. And, if you want this outfit, get a job and pay for it with your own money."

"Oh my god, did my mom hire you or something?" I said frustrated.

"Can you just listen to me for a second? You are being stuck up little brat right now. Are you mad at your mom because she said 'no' to the outfit or because she 'implied' that the outfit didn't fit properly?"

"Oh, you mean that I am not as skinny as Britney Spears? Yes, that. Listen, I already have enough problems as it is being a deformed kid, I really don't need anyone telling me that I am fat too." I said as I started to cry again.

"Lindsay, you are not fat. You are beautiful and perfect, well, the attitude could be adjusted, just the way you are. Your mom knows that too, but she also knows that you are just a girl, not yet a woman."

P started to laugh.

"What are you talking about?" I asked her confused.

"Oh, you'll find out later. Anyways, she is just trying to protect you from any possible haters. Whereas she could have been nicer about it, she does have the best intentions for you. Plus, no one really looks like Britney Spears and that picture is probably Photoshopped."

"What's Photoshopped?" I asked confused again.

"Never mind that. Lindsay, you are you and no one else and that is your power. Never compare yourself to anyone else, especially a celebrity, and especially not Britney Spears, okay?" She said as she grabbed my arms.

"Are you okay now? Did this help? Do you need a hug?" Asked P.

"I'm good," I said as I pulled away.

"Good because I'm not really good at the touchy-feely stuff anyway."

"I'm okay, you can go now," I said as I looked back at her.

"Ok then, until next time." She said with a wave.

"I hope there won't be a next time." I said.

"Sooner than you think." She said as she disappeared.

I heard a knock on the dressing room door.

"Linz, are you okay? You are taking a lot of time to change in there." My mom asked.

I opened the door as she looked at me and could tell I had been crying.

"Come here." She said as she hugged me.

"I love you, you know that, right?" She asked me.

I shook my head yes.

"If you want the outfit, I will get it for you." She said.

"No, it's okay. Can we try on a few more things?" I asked.

My mom smiled at me and said, "Absolutely. I found a few things that I think would look so cute on you."

We spent a few more hours at the mall and I found a few things that would work for school clothes that my mom and I both agreed on.

Having P around wasn't so bad after all; I mean, she did talk me off the ledge in the dressing room, and some of the stuff she said made sense. It was kind of nice to have someone I could talk to about stuff, even if she was made up in my head.

The next day I decided to go for a jog in the neighborhood. The dressing room was more than enough motivation for me to get outside and be more active. I did exercise, but my love of food typically overpowered my physical efforts. So, I put a CD in my Discman and put my headphones on and started to run.

I was doing well, for the first half-mile, then my body turned on me and I was having a hard time breathing. When I stopped, I looked around and I was at the lake where I met Billy for the first time. I decided to take a break and have a seat at Billy's bench and watch the ducks.

I felt someone pull at my headphones and ask, "What are you listening to?"

I jumped.

"Oh! Fuck Billy, you can't do that to me. You'll give me a heart attack" I said catching my breath.

He laughed, "You like my bench huh?"

"No, I just took a break from my jog," I said trying not to seem interested in the conversation.

"You never answered my question." He replied.

"I'm sorry, I was in the middle of being terrified. What did you ask me?"

"What are you listening to?" He asked again.

I let out a pretentious laugh and said, "Oh, you wouldn't know them."

"I am a huge music lover, try me." He said with confidence.

"It's Depeche Mode," I replied looking to see if the name resonated.

"Nope, don't know them. Are they a band?" He asked.

"I would say group; they are a new wave band from the '80s, but their new music is better than their old stuff. I'm listening to their new album, *Ultra*."

He smiled, "Ultra huh? I'm going to have to listen."

"Yeah, you can get their album at Best—"

But before I could say the rest, Billy already had the other headphone up to his ear listening.

"I like it. Very electronic." He said.

"What kind of music do you listen to?" I asked him.

"Pretty much everything, well, everything except Depec—(he couldn't pronounce it), but Country is my favorite."

I laughed.

"Country? Oh no." I said.

"What's wrong with Country music?" He asked.

"It's just so twangy." I snarled.

"Yeah, yeah, but there's so much more to it than that?"

"Oh really, what is it that you like so much about it?" I asked being pompous.

He put his hand on top of mine as I looked at him confused and then he put my hand over his heart.

"Country music is either happy or sad, but either way it comes from here. You know exactly what the song is about and how they felt when they wrote the song. It's actually really beautiful—like you." He said as he looked deeply into my eyes.

I immediately pulled away and jumped up.

"I have to get back to my jog now," I said nervously.

"Okay, I'll see you around then?" He asked.

"Yeah, maybe," I said as I ran off.

Ew, was he trying to hit on me? Did he know I was only 13? He was like 15 and that was just gross.

"What was that back there?" P asked.

"Where do you come from?" I asked.

"Everywhere!" She said smiling.

"Ugh, you are so annoying. Why are you here?" I asked.

"Well, I just witnessed little mister getting handsy back there and I wanted to get all of the juicy deets." P said extremely giddy.

"There are no deets. We were just talking about music and he put his hand on mine and then onto his chest. I don't want to talk about this right now, I'm trying to work out", I responded trying to avoid her questioning.

Then she gasped.

"What? What's wrong?" I asked concerned.

"What if he likes you?" She asked as she grabbed my t-shirt.

"Ew, no," I responded.

"Ew? You don't like him? He's really cute and seems really sweet and totally into you. I don't know, I think it could be a thing." She said rambling.

"It will not be a 'thing'. I don't like him like that; I don't even know if I like him as a friend, but it's definitely not like that." I said.

"Okay, but just watch it because you don't want it to get messy." P said.

"Please leave me alone," I said as I started to jog faster.

"As you wish Master!" She said as she gave me a salute and jogged off.

She was right, I did have to watch it; I couldn't have him thinking that he had a shot with me when I wanted was to friends. I had to draw the line in the sand and make it very clear to him that we were only going to be friends.

It turned out to be more of a difficult task than I thought because my mom became close with Billy's mom, so we hung out more and more for the remainder of the summer. We went to the movies, waterpark, sporting events, etc. together and I couldn't avoid him.

The summer was coming to an end and school started soon, so I asked to have Maggie over for the night, and of course, my brother asked Billy to stay over too.

"Lindsay, can we go for a walk?" Billy asked me after dinner.

"Sure," I said confused as to why he wanted to walk with me in the dark.

The night was warm and muggy, being as it was Florida in August that wasn't so shocking, but even at night, it was unrelentingly hot.

We were quiet for the first few feet, neither of us said anything to one another.

"So, you ready for school?" I asked him, trying to make small talk to get the conversation going.

"I like you." He blurted out.

"What?" I asked.

"You know that I like you, like you like you, more than just a friend." He said as we stopped in the middle of the road.

I stood there not knowing what to say. Where was P when I needed her?

"Billy, I just turned thirteen and my dad won't let me date anyone." I lied.

Why couldn't I just be honest with him? Even though I didn't have feelings for him as he did for me, I still didn't want to break his heart.

"Oh." He said as he put his head down.

"Listen, maybe when I get a little bit older, we can see how we feel? But can we please still be friends?" I asked.

Why didn't I just pull out a dagger and jab it straight through his heart while I was at it?

"Yeah, sure." He said choking up. "I made you this." He added as he handed me a tape.

I looked at it and it said, "Songs for The Most Beautiful Girl in the World".

"Thank you!" I said as I threw my arms around him and hugged him.

"Do you want to go listen to it?" I asked.

"Oh no. I think you should listen to that on your own and I think I'm going to go home." He said as he started to walk away.

"You're not staying the night?" I asked.

"No, tell your brother I'll call him later." He said as he walked away.

What just happened?

"Wow, that was brutal."

"P! Where the hell were you? I really could have used your help back there." I said frustrated.

"Oh no, that was all you, compadre!" She said with her hands up.

"What was I supposed to do?" I asked.

"Um, I don't know, tell the truth maybe?" She responded. "Why did you lie to him like that? He didn't deserve that." She added.

"I know. I just couldn't; I think I heard his actual heart-breaking in his chest and it's all my fault." I said as I slid down and sat on the curb with my head in my hands.

"It's okay, you can't help how you feel. If you don't like him, you don't like him—I mean, I don't know why you don't like him because he is so freakin' adorable."

"If you like him so much why don't you go out with him?" I said annoyed.

"Um ew, I'm like way older than he is, gross Lindsay." She said as she sat next to me.

"Why is everything happening to me? I didn't ask for this; I didn't ask for him to like me and now I feel bad. Why do I feel so bad?" I asked her.

"I can't answer that for you, only you know the answer to that question, but what I can tell you is to just be a really good friend to him right now and be gentle."

I nodded and looked down at the tape Billy made me.

"He made you a mixed tape? Oh my god, that is the sweetest thing I think I've ever seen!" P said gasping.

"You're not helping."

"Sorry." She said as she shushed herself.

That night I put the tape in and listened to it beginning to end, end to the beginning. They were all country songs, his favorite songs, and songs that reminded him of me. I opened the case up again and he put a note that read, "I'm a little bit country, and you're a little bit rock n' roll."

# Chapter 6: Smells Like Teen Spirit

It was finally that time of year when most kids my age dreaded, back to school time. I, on the other hand, was unlike the other kids my age and loved going to school, except it was a year unlike any other. I was starting 8th grade at a new school, a private Baptist school nonetheless, but I had a positive mindset and that was all I needed, or so I thought.

I woke up early excited and anxious, took a shower, and got dressed in my brand-new clothes. I felt like a million bucks. I decided in my mind that I wasn't going to be a push-over anymore, that I was going to own my power and just be myself. I had a newly found sense of confidence going into the new school year, and I liked it.

"I made you breakfast." My mom said as she handed me a plate of eggs.

"Ew, mom, you know I don't eat breakfast," I said snarling my nose at the scrambled eggs.

"I don't care, you're going to eat them; you need brain food." She said as she pushed the plate closer to me.

"Fine," I said as I pretended to eat them and gave them to the dog instead.

My brother and I piled into the car as our mom drove us to school.

On our way there we saw a woman riding her bicycle.

"I bet that's one of your teachers." My mom said as she looked back at the woman in the rear-view mirror.

"I hope not, she looks like the Wicked Witch of the West." My brother said as my mom made the *Wizard of Oz* sound effect.

I was in a car with children.

When the car got closer to the school my anxiety began to set in.

"Okay, you two please behave. I packed your lunches for you. I love you!" My mom shouted from inside the car as the other kids arriving overheard.

"Aw, we love you mom!", said Bobby as he walked into the school.

I walked into my new classroom and there was so much hustle and bustle; kids laughing and chatting, but as soon as they saw me, they got quiet.

"Alright class, I have assigned you all a locker to put your things in, please find yours quickly and have a seat so we can get started." Said an older lady.

I found my locker, but I couldn't get the damn thing to open and I didn't want to be late, so I just carried all of my books in my backpack.

"Class, my name is Ms. Green, no I'm not married, so don't call me Mrs. or I will give you immediate detention, you hear? I am your homeroom teacher and your Biology teacher, oh joy. I love science and the TV show *ER*. Now that you know all about me, I'd like to get to know all of you. Stand up, say your name, and one thing about you. Just one thing, I don't need a biography." She said enthusiastically.

The class took turns alphabetically, and since my last name began with "Y", I was always last.

It was finally my turn.

"Hi, my name is Lindsay and I'm a Leo; I like NSYN*C and will most likely marry Justin Timberlake. He's an Aquarius so Leo's and Aquarius' are highly compatible with one another—"

Ms. Green interrupted.

"Okay Ms. Cleo, I think that's enough for today."

To which I responded, "Call me now for your free reading".

The class went into hysterics and I was an instant favorite among my peers.

Making people laugh was a trick I learned throughout my transient years, a trick that served me well, because if you make people laugh you make their guard come down and it's easier for people to want to get to know you.

"Looks like we already have our class clown", Ms. Green said as she gave me the side-eye.

"More like the class crown." I snarked back to her.

I looked at school like a giant game of *Risk*; you have for allies, always know your opponents, and be ten steps ahead of everyone else. It was a piece of cake.

The bell rang and a few girls from my class ran up to me.

"Sit by us in History okay?" They asked.

"Yeah sure," I said as I gathered my books.

"Ms. Young, a quick word?" Asked Ms. Green.

Ugh oh, here it comes, the power struggle speech that I heard time and time again from teachers all across America about how they are the teacher and I am the student so I must comply.

"Ms. Young, I can already tell you are an extremely intelligent student, and you are going to give me a run for my money this year. So why don't we just make a pact that you won't run my classroom and I will make sure you get a good grade in my class". She said with a smile.

"Sounds like a plan," I said as we shook hands.

I already had my teacher wrapped around my finger, but there was only one person I was interested in seeing, but I couldn't find him anywhere.

It was lunchtime and the upper grades (6-12) had the same lunch time, so I had my eyes open and waited to see the 9th graders arrive.

"Ugh, I can't get the straw in my Capri Sun! Lindsay, can you try?" One of my classmates asked me.

"Sure, give it here," I said as I tried to puncture a hole in the juice bag.

"Got it!" I said as I was about to hand it back.

"Got you!" A voice said from behind as they grabbed my waist.

I jumped up in shock, spilling the Capri Sun all over myself in the process.

"God Damnit!" I yelled as I turned around and saw Zach.

"Ms. Young and Mr. Wells, in my office now!" yelled the Pastor.

"I'm sorry Lindsay, just follow my lead, Mr. Pastor and I know each other well," Zach said as we walked together to his office.

"Uh oh, already sent to the principal's office on the first day, not good Lindsay." P said popping out of nowhere.

"Shut up!" I whispered.

"What?" Asked Zach.

"Oh, nothing," I said as I looked over at P.

"Really Lindsay, this guy? I think Billy is cuter." She said looking over at Zach.

"Will you just go away, please?" I pleaded.

We got to the Pastor's office.

"You two have a seat please." He said pointing at the two seats in front of his desk.

"Mr. Wells, I didn't think I would be seeing you again this soon." The Pastor said looking at Zach.

"Pastor, I'm sorry, it's my fault. I accidentally scared her, and it won't happen again." Zach pleaded.

"Mr. Wells let me put this in a way that you can understand, if I see you in this office again for any reason other than you saw Jesus walking the halls, I will suspend you so fast."

"I promise Pastor, you won't." He reiterated.

"Mr. Wells, you may go. I need to talk to Ms. Young now." The pastor said as he excused Zach.

"Ms. Young, I have to say I am very disappointed in you. When I met with your mother, she told me how you and your brother were outstanding students, but that's not what I witnessed out there, saying the Lord's name in vain like that".

"Pastor, I apologize for my actions, there is no excuse for it, but it will never happen again, I promise". I said in a somber tone.

"Alright, this is your one pass, but Ms. Young you don't need to be hanging around Mr. Wells, he is trouble and you don't want to be any part of that, do you understand?" He asked.

Um, no, but I replied with, "Yes, sir."

I walked out of the room and Zach was waiting for me.

"Lindsay, I'm sorry about that, no one wants to get sent to the principal's office, especially on the first day of school." He said.

"Well, there's no one I'd rather be sent there with than you," I said with a wink.

I headed to the bathroom to see if I could salvage my new shirt after the juice fiasco.

"You're not going to listen to the pastor, are you?" P asked popping out of thin air again.

"What? About Zach?" I asked her.

"Yeah, he's obviously bad news. Two people have told you this already, but no, you're in love." She said taunting me.

"Ugh, no I'm not. I just like to make up my own assumptions about people and not have other's shoved down my throat, okay?"

"Whatever. All I'm saying is follow your gut intuition." She said.

"Well, my gut is telling me that you need to go and leave me alone," I said frustrated.

"Okay, but don't say I didn't tell you so." She said as she disappeared.

Such an annoying, creepy bitch.

The rest of the day was uneventful, except when I walked into math class and saw the *Wizard of Oz* lady who was *apparently* my teacher.

"My name is Ms. Maria." She said quietly.

I overheard the kids next to me whispering.

"She smells really bad." They said laughing and giggling.

You could tell she was nervous and didn't know how to handle her classroom. These kids were going to eat her alive.

The day ended with my mom picking up my brother and me; you could always tell it was her because we could hear the Cranberries blasting from her 3000 GT.

"How was your day kids?" She said extremely excited.

"It was fine." My brother said omitting any emotion.

"Well, mine was very exciting," I said.

"That's good, what happened?" She asked me curiously.

"Oh, well, I made a few new acquaintances, I like my teachers for the most part, and I got sent to the principal's office."

"You did what?" She yelled.

"It was nothing, just a pure misunderstanding. I didn't get in trouble." I said brushing off the incident.

"Lindsay, I swear. Your dad and I are paying a lot of money for you two to go to that school so you're not subject to Florida's public-school system. The least you could do is behave, please."

"Of course, it will never happen again," I said.

"It better not or I will beat you like I did after the school bus incident." She said.

Listen, my mom never beat me, but she did give me an ass whooping whenever I needed one, and the school bus incident was no exception.

The "School Bus Incident" as my family later called it would go down in infamy as the day I royally got my ass beat by my mother.

I was ten years old and in 5th grade at the time of the incident. My best friend at the time, Brittney, and I rode the bus together every afternoon. If you have ever had the insurmountable pleasure of ever riding on a school bus then you know the indelible scar it can leave on a young child and what an incredible shit-show it was too.

On this particular bus ride, Brittney thought it would be cool to write out our names in white-out on the back of the seat in front of us. Me, being the gullible dumb ass that I was, agreed with this idiot plan.

While I was sitting in class learning about the eco-system, I heard my name called over the school intercom to go to the principal's office.

I was scared out of my mind thinking about the things I could have possibly done to get me there, but never thought it could be the graffiti on the bus.

"You have vandalized school property." The principal scorned.

Vandalize? I'd never even heard of that word until then.

"No, I didn't." I adamantly disagreed.

"Oh? Shall we go take a look then?" He asked.

A field trip? Was that really necessary?

There it was in all white, "Lindsay sits here".

"It could be another Lindsay," I argued.

"Really? Ms. Young, you better admit to it now. I have already called your mother and told her I would suspend you if you don't tell me the truth, and you're lucky we won't press charges either. I would be more afraid of what your mother is going to do when you get home today." The principal said crossing his arms and looking at me like a hardened criminal.

To be honest, I was more terrified of my mother than any other authority figure. The thought of what my mom was going to do when I got off the bus that day scared me more than anything, so I started to cry and confessed to my crime…of being stupid.

I wasn't suspended or sent off to Juvey, but I might as well have been because I knew I was dead when the day was over.

When the bus stopped, I looked out the window and saw my mom standing beside the car with her arms folded. She was ready for me.

I slowly walked towards her with tears filling up in my eyes.

"Get in the car!" She yelled.

Yep, she was pissed.

She hit me from the time I got out of the car until the grand finale in my bedroom with me pleading, "Mom, I'm sorry. I'll never do it again!"

I will pause here and let you know that I was fine. Did I deserve a spanking? Yes. Do I condone this kind of punishment? I think it is up to the parent's discretion, but I do think there were better ways she could have handled this particular situation without getting physical. I know it is hard to fathom, but kids still got spankings in the 1990s. I learned my lesson and never vandalized another thing.

That evening I was getting ready for bed and P suddenly interrupted me while I was brushing my teeth.

"Hi, there!" She yelled causing me to spit my toothpaste all over the mirror.

"Could you stop popping up like this and scaring me?" I asked.

"Sorry, I can't really predict when I show up, I just kind of do."

"Well, it's really annoying," I said as I walked past her and back to my bedroom.

"How was your first day at school? Well, besides being sent to the principal's office." P asked me.

"It was surprisingly good. I made some new friends and I like all of my classes, so we'll see how it goes." I said optimistically.

"Totally. I love that for you. Just let me know if you need anything. I'm here to guide you, remember?" She asked as she sat on the edge of the bed.

"I remember. I better go to sleep so I can get a full 8 hours of beauty rest, so you have to go now. I can't have you watching me while I sleep, that is so creepy." I said kicking her up and out of my bed.

She laughed and said, "Okay, okay, you don't have to tell me twice."

She turned around and I said, "Than—", but before I could say the words my mom opened my door.

"Linz? Who are you talking to?" She asked peaking her head into my room.

"No one, just myself," I said.

"Oh, well, lights out." She said.

"I love you mom," I said.

"I love you too, now get some sleep." She said as she closed my door.

The next few weeks at school were uneventful, but I was stepping into my own and making new friends in my class. A couple of girls, Deanna and Roxette, were also huge

N*SYNC fans so we bonded over our obsession with them. I also made a few new friends when I tried out for the JV volleyball team.

I was never a "sports" girl, never really liked it, and I never like joining big groups either, but if I was going to get to see all of the cute boys, Zach included, then I had to be on a sports team, so I assumed that volleyball would be the easiest.

I was surprised how fast I was able to pick up the game since I had never played before in my life, but I was pretty good at it and I secretly enjoyed it.

When I made the team, I was so excited; they announced everyone's name at the end of practice in the gym. I was jumping up and down with my friends when I heard a voice.

"Great job, congratulations Linz!" Zach said as he hugged me.

I saw the look on the other girl's faces when he left.

"You know Zach?" Deanna asked me.

"Yeah, he's friends with my brother and I'm friends with his sister Maggie," I said as I look off my knee pads.

"Oh my god, he is so cute. Do you think he would be interested in going out with one of us?" Roxette asked me.

"I don't know, you could ask him," I suggested to her.

"Oh, I could never, but maybe you could ask him for me?" She asked.

I laughed, "I really don't want to get involved." I said as I grabbed my backpack.

"Hey Linz, Maggie wanted me to ask if you wanted to come over tonight? Mom's making tacos?" Zach asked from across the room.

"I have to ask my mom, but if she says yes, then I'll be there!" I yelled back.

"Cool, see ya then!" He yelled.

"Oh my god Linz, you're going over to his house? You are so cool." They both squealed in excitement.

I asked my mom about going to Maggie's house for dinner and she said yes.

I was finally invited into Maggie and Zach's layer; they had been over at my house numerous times, but this was the first time I was ever invited into their home and I was so excited and so nervous.

I rang the doorbell and Maggie answered. I could smell the tacos cooking in the kitchen.

"Come in, my mom is making the tacos now, but we can chill in my room until it's done," Maggie said as she led me down the hall into her room.

It was cute and yellow everything. Their Spaniel came into the room to say 'hi' to me too.

"I was looking everywhere for you!" Zach said as he peeked in the room.

"She just got here," Maggie said annoyed.

He laughed, "I was talking about the dog, but I guess I found you too." He said as he looked at me and winked.

Oh my god, was he flirting with me?

"I hope you brought your bathing suit because we're going to go night swimming after dinner." He said as he left the room with the dog.

"Ugh, he is so annoying," Maggie said as she shut her door.

"Does he do this when all of your friends come over?" I asked her.

'You're the only friend I've had over, so I guess so." She said laughing.

We listened to some music until we were called to dinner. It was just Shirley, Maggie, Zach, and I. Their dad was nowhere to be seen.

"Mrs. Wells these tacos are delicious," I said.

"We have taco Tuesday every week, you are invited any time." She said as she popped the top off a Corona beer.

"Yes, any time." Zach chimed in.

"Zach is going to help me with these dishes, but Maggie said you guys wanted to go swimming. I turned the pool lights on back there, just be careful and no running. I don't want anyone to slip and fall, dear god."

The dreaded showing off the bathing suit time. I was thirteen, already started my period, and was developing boobs at an alarming rate. No one my age or in my class had big boobs like me and I hated them. I would tape them up with Duct tape so they would stand out, but I couldn't do that in a bathing suit.

Thankfully, it was just Maggie and me, so I felt comfortable, that was until Zach decided to join us.

His body looked like Michelangelo sculpted it out of marble. He had washboard abs and pecs straight out of an Abercrombie advert. He did a cannonball into the pool, I guess to show-off, but Maggie was not impressed. When he came out of the water it was like slow motion as he shook his hair back and forth.

"I have to go to the bathroom. Lindsay, you have my full permission to drown him while I'm gone." She said as she jumped out of the pool.

Shit, I was all alone with the most beautiful boy I'd ever seen, and I didn't know what to do. I went under to wet my hair again and came back up slowly. I opened my eyes, and he was just staring at me.

"What is it?" I asked him.

He had that Cheshire grin on his face again and said, "Right then, when you came out of the water, you looked like Denise Richards in *Wild Things*."

I'd never seen the movie, probably because I was too young, but I understood his reference from a movie preview I saw.

I was blushing and didn't know how to respond. So, I just splashed him with water, and he retaliated.

When looked down I noticed that my bikini top was white and you could see right through it, nipples and all. Did Zach see them? I gasped and he asked, "What? What is it?"

I responded with the only thing I could think of, "I think I lost my earring."

"Oh, let me go down and see if I could find it."

When he was underwater, I jumped out of the pool and immediately wrapped myself up in a towel.

He popped back up, "I didn't see anything."

"Oh, that's okay, I'm sure it will turn up," I said.

Maggie came back out and saw me in my towel.

"Are you done swimming?" She asked.

"Yeah, I should probably be heading back home, you know, school night."

"I can walk you back home," Zach said as he slowly stepped out of the pool, with the water clenching his tight body.

"Um, no, it's cool, I rode my bike," I said as I grabbed my clothes and practically ran out of their house.

The next day I was in gym class finishing up the girls vs boys dodgeball game when I heard our teacher's whistle.

"Everyone, gather around!" He yelled.

There was a cute, tall, dark-headed boy standing next to him.

"Everyone, this is Gabriel, a new student from Washington state."

## Chapter 7: God Must Have Spent A Little More Time on You

"Everyone, give Gabriel a big warm welcome; he will be with the 10th graders, but you might see him at lunch or in study hall." Said Ms. Green.

He waved at everyone before he was led upstairs to the high school classrooms.

"OMG, what do you think of the new boy Linz?" Asked Roxette as she clung onto me.

"He seems nice," I said trying not to pay too much attention to her questions.

"No silly, do you think he's cute? I think he's super cute." She said excitedly as we headed to the locker room.

"He's okay. He's no Brad Pitt or Justin Timberlake." I said as I rolled my eyes.

"Or Zach", teased Deanna.

"C'mon guys, he's just a friend," I said as I shoved my books in my backpack and headed to my next class.

"You can't tell us that if he asked you out today, you wouldn't go out with him?" Asked Roxette.

"I really don't know, and I am already late for class," I said as walked away.

Roxette and Dee looked at each other and said at the same time, "She totally would."

The next week was uneventful, but I did notice Gabriel and Zach hanging around one another a lot. I guess Zach decided to take him under his wing and show him the ropes, but I also wondered how The Pastor felt about that due to his disdain for Zach.

"Who's the new smoke-show?" P asked as she popped up in the girl's bathroom as I was changing for gym class.

"His name is Gabriel, but Zach said he goes by 'G'. His parents are old, wealthy types who moved to Florida to retire."

"Wow, you seem to know a lot about him."

"What are you implying?" I asked her.

"Nothing, it was just an observation." She said as she tried to brush my hair.

"Please don't," I said as I grabbed the brush from her.

"You know, I do know a lot about fashion and beauty, so if you ever want some tips, I am here for you." She said as she messed in someone else's make-up bag.

"I don't, but thanks for the offer," I said as I rushed out of the room before anyone noticed that I was talking to myself.

I should have taken P up on her offer. I had no style what-so-ever, but it also didn't help that I was a teenager in the '90s, and let's face it, the fashion totally sucked ass.

Scrunchies, JNCO jeans, ugly Abercrombie sweaters; yes, I wore all of it. The fact was, fashion wasn't at the forefront of my mind because I hated my changing body, I honestly didn't want anyone to see it. I hid behind oversized sweaters and jeans but thought I was cool because I could hang with the boys. I was in desperate need of a make-over, but I wasn't about to ask P for one.

I was in study hall when I heard Dee whisper in my ear, "This is from Zach".

With a huge smile on her face she handed me a note that read:

*Jet Ski with G this weekend?*

*-Zach* ♡

I looked up and Zach and Gabriel were both staring at me. I nodded my head "yes" and they both celebrated.

"What did the note say?" Asked Dee.

"Zach asked me to go jet skiing with him and Gabriel this weekend."

She squealed so loud with excitement.

"Shhhh," I said trying not to draw too much attention.

"Holy crap, you are the coolest girl in the school. The two most popular guys asked you to hang out with them this weekend. Ugh, can I be you?" She asked.

"It's really not a big deal, and my mom will probably say no anyway," I said.

I was wrong about that.

Later that evening I discovered that my mom had been plotting this the whole time.

"I met Gabriel's mom the other day and she, Shirley, and I went out for brunch. I really like her. She invited us all out to the lake this weekend to jet ski and you are going." My mom said sternly.

"I get no say in this?" I asked annoyed.

"You don't want to go have fun at the lake and jet ski? With Maggie? And cute boys? That Gabriel is adorable." My mom said with a wink.

"It's fine. I just don't know which bathing suit I want to wear." I said as my anxiety started to build.

"I would say one that covers up your unflattering parts."

"Mom, that's mean," I said almost in tears.

"I am just being honest. No boy is going to want to be around a girl with chubs hanging out." She said seriously.

"I honestly can't stand you sometimes," I said as I started to cry and ran into my room. I started blasting my new 98 Degrees CD as loud as I could.

"Your mom again?" P asked as she saw me crying into my pillow.

"Who else? My dad never says anything mean to me like that, it's just her."

"I know it's hard because it's your mom, but she thinks she means well. You just have to love your body no matter what anyone says. You are so beautiful Lindsay, you know that right?"

"No, I'm not. I'm a fat freak." I said as I cried harder into my pillow.

"Who said that? You did. You are filling your mind up with nonsense."

"It's not though. I just watched a movie and it had someone who had a cleft-lip, and they were an inbred freak, and that is what people see when they look at me too—a monster. A chubby, ugly, monster."

"Oh, baby girl, you are not any of those things. You are a beautiful girl, a smart girl, a funny girl. You just have to realize it, and tune-out all that white noise in your head. You are probably the most confident girl I've ever met and the most self-assured. You are going to rule the world, but you have to believe it. Come here." P said as she pulled me out of my pillow sanctuary and gave me a long hug.

"Thank you," I said as I wiped the tear from my eyes.

"I mean, that's why I'm here." She said with a wink as she gazed at my *Labyrinth* movie poster on my wall.

"Man, David Bowie is incredible, huh? Appreciate him, go to one of his concerts, you won't be disappointed." She said just staring at his face in awe of him.

"I'm okay now," I said as I heard a knock at my door.

"Right on time." P said with a smile and disappeared.

"Linz, who are you talking to?" My mom asked.

"Myself," I said trying not to show too much emotion.

"Well, I wanted to come in and say that I was a little too harsh. I just know how mean kids can be and you already have so many obstacles in your way; I have good intentions."

"I know, but you have to watch how you say things sometimes because it really does hurt my feelings," I said trying not to cry.

"I know, and I will from now on, I promise." She said as she hugged me.

"I love you so much Lindsay and I don't want anyone to hurt you because you know what I'll do to them if they do." She said laughing.

I laughed too because I knew she would beat anyone's ass who tried to hurt me.

"How about you and I go pick out an appropriate swimsuit tomorrow after school?" She asked trying to compromise.

"Sounds like a plan," I said.

I was never a skinny girl, unlike the other girls in my class, and add big boobs and braces on top of that and I felt like a total outsider, but what I lacked in beauty I made up for in personality, at least that's what I kept telling myself.

The next day my mom and I went swimsuit shopping which was not helping in the self-confidence department at all, but I had to get something for my weekend of "fun" with the boys.

We compromised on a cute red monokini that zipped up in the front; I had the cleavage so I thought I might as well use that to my advantage.

The day finally arrived as my mom, brother, and I headed to the lake to begin our day of fun in the sun.

I could see Zach, Maggie, and Shirley getting out of their car, and Zach took his shirt off to spray on some sunscreen. What a sight to be seen; the way his six-pack glistened as he slowly rubbed his body down.

"Earth to Lindsay, are you coming?" My brother asked me, interrupting my swooning.

"Yeah, yeah, yeah, I'm coming," I said as I tried to exit the car as gracefully and sexy as possible, even though I had no idea what any of those things meant.

"Linz!" I hear Maggie yell.

"I love your bathing suit! Did you see they have the jet skis and the tubes?" She asked me way too excited.

"Oh, fun," I said trying to sound enthusiastic.

Water and I didn't go well together, but I was going to give it the old Girl Scout try and hopefully spend some quality time with Zach.

"Hey, Linz, like the suit. Ready to get wet?" He asked.

Too late for that.

"You're not one of those girls who freak out if their hair gets wet are you?" Asked Gabriel as he walked up to Zach and me.

Zach smiled as I responded, "Not at all." I said as I threw my towel over my shoulder and walked past him.

Of course, I was! Who was I kidding? I was such a girly girl and the thought of being wet all day sounded appalling to me.

Gabriel and Zach walked up to the picnic tables where everyone was laying down their stuff and applying sunscreen.

"Ok, Zach and I are going to try out the first jet ski, make sure everything is running properly, if the girls want to go out, my mom said she will take them. We have skis and tubes if you want to try those out too. Let's have some fun today!" Gabriel said trying to pump everyone up, I guess.

"Do you want to go out with Karen?" Maggie asked me.

"Um yeah sure. Let me just put this sunscreen on and we'll be ready to go." I said struggling with getting my back and shoulders.

"Here let me help you," Zach said as he grabbed the sunscreen bottle and began to rub it on my shoulders and back.

His touch sent electric bolts down my body and I didn't want him to stop.

"Ok, Zach, I think she's good. C'mon Linz, let's get out there!" Maggie said as she grabbed my hand and we ran down the hill to the lake where Gabriel's mom, Karen, was waiting.

"Hi girls, I have some safety rules for you. Always wear a life vest, try these on and make sure they're snug. I am the only driver, not that I don't trust you, I just don't want to be liable if anything happens. Don't tip over the jet ski, it can be dangerous if it falls on top of you, but most of all, have fun!"

We got our life vests on and made our way onto the jet ski.

It was Karen, me, and Maggie in the back.

I could see my mom at the edge of the water waving with a camcorder in her hand.

"Have fun girls!" I heard her yell.

I also saw Zach and Gabriel waving at us from their jet ski.

We started slow and then Karen picked up the speed.

All I could think about was not tipping the jet ski because I didn't want to get wet, and there were alligators in the water—it was Florida.

I heard Maggie laughing and screaming behind me; she seemed to be having a good time, but I was still freaked out.

We were in the water for a good 30 minutes, but I was ready to get back on land.

"Looks like you girls had some much fun!" Shirley said greeting us with a Corona in hand.

"Want to ride with me next?" Gabriel asked me.

"Only if Maggie comes too," I said trying to make it obvious that I didn't want to be alone with Gabriel.

It's not that I didn't like him, don't get me wrong, he was hella cute, but I just didn't know him, and he came across as kind of pompous to me which I didn't like very much.

"Yeah sure." He said as he helped me get on the jet ski.

Maggie already signaled to me that she didn't want to be in the middle; I guess she didn't want to have to put her arms around him. So, I had to be the one to do it.

Gabriel looked back to me and asked, "Are you ready?"

"I guess so," I said.

"Hold on tight!" He said as he pushed the throttle as hard as he could, and we went flying.

Maggie and I were screaming at the top of our lungs as I clung onto him for dear life.

"Don't tip the jet ski!", yelled Gabriel.

"What?", I could barely hear him.

"Don't tip the---"

But before he could finish his sentence, I could feel the water hit my face.

I immediately popped out of the water.

"Are you okay?" Gabriel asked.

"I'm fine. Maggie are you okay?" I asked her.

She gave me a thumbs up.

Gabriel swam over to the overturned jet ski and pushed it upright quickly.

"Hurry, you don't want the gators to get you." He said as he held out his hand.

I helped Maggie get on and we headed back toward the picnic tables.

When we got off the jet ski none of us looked happy.

"Uh oh, you guys got soaked, what happened?" Asked Karen.

"These two tipped the jet ski," Gabriel said blaming Maggie and me.

"Well, maybe we wouldn't have if you weren't driving like a madman," I said as I threw my life vest at him and stormed off.

I dried off a little in the sun and I saw a shadow standing over me.

"Do you want to go out with me? On the jet ski, I mean." Asked Zach.

"I don't know, I think I'm pretty much done after tipping the jet ski," I said blocking the sun with my hand.

"The best thing to do when you fall off is getting right back on. C'mon." He said as he reached out his hand.

I guess Karen and Gabriel allowed Zach to drive one of their precious skis solo.

Zach helped me onto the ski as I held onto him tightly. He looked back at me and smiled.

"You ready Precious?" He asked.

"Precious huh?" I asked him.

"Yeah, you're too precious to hurt." He said as he slowly took off, unlike Gabriel.

We were jumping waves and laughing so hard, and I was having the best time, then he stopped the jet ski in the middle of the water and we just sat there.

"Everything okay?" I asked him.

"Yeah, I just thought we could just have a moment." He said as he turned around to face me.

"You having fun?" He asked.

"I am now."

"We don't really get to talk much at school and we're always with our families outside of school, so I thought we could catch up. Have you gotten to any more trouble since, well, you and I were sent to the Pastor's office?" He laughed.

"No, I'm trying to be on my best behavior, you know, since people are watching me now."

"Oh, they are, especially if you're hanging out with me." He said as he looked down.

"Did you used to get in a lot of trouble?" I asked.

"Yeah, I wasn't the best behaved, but I think I'm passed all that now."

"That's good to hear; I always love a reformed bad boy," I said shocked that something like that would ever come out of my mouth.

He smiled, "So, I heard you turned Billy down."

"You know Billy?" I asked.

"Yeah, we've been friends since we were kids. He really likes you."

"Well, I think he's a great guy, but just not the guy for me," I said looking right into his piercing blue eyes.

Then, his hand brushed my cheek. Oh my god! Is this it? Is he going to finally kiss me? The butterflies were fluttering all over my stomach.

He smiled and said, "Well, you know I've always got your back and I'm sure that guy is out there. How about we head back? I think our moms are making lunch."

He turned back around and started up the jet ski again.

What the fuck was that? I felt crushed like someone jammed their fist right through my chest and pulled my heart out. I felt like jumping into the water and having the alligators eat me alive.

I started crying, but I was still wet from the jet ski so you couldn't tell.

I was quiet for the rest of the day and I didn't want to eat or participate in anything; I just wanted to go home.

I went to the park bathroom and P was there waiting, as I expected.

"What the hell is his problem?" She asked me.

I was shocked because I was expecting the typical P response that everything will be okay and it'll all work out, but she was being cool.

"I know right? I was totally expecting him to kiss me, but it was like he freaked out or something."

"Forget him, girl, there are so many cute guys. What about Gabriel? He's super cute." She said putting on lipstick in the mirror.

"Why are you always putting on make-up? Where do you go where you have to wear make-up all of the time?" I asked her curiously.

"Um, one I can't tell you, and two, who says you need an excuse to wear make-up? I wear it because I love it." She said being very sassy.

"Ok, just asking. Also, Gabriel is just a stuck-up snob and I would never like someone like that." I said.

"You sure about that?" She asked.

"You are being really annoying today, can you please disappear and go back to wherever you're from?"

"Ugh gladly!" She said as she disappeared.

I washed my hands and headed out of the restroom and was met by Gabriel.

"Who were you talking to in there?" He asked.

"No one," I said secretly freaking out.

"I was in the men's bathroom and heard you. You really think I'm a stuck-up snob, huh?" He asked as he walked away from me.

Great, now he hates me. The day had turned into a royal mess and I was ready to go home.

On the car ride home, my mom looked over at me in the passenger's side, "You're awfully quiet. Did you have fun today?" She asked.

"It was a blast," I said as I turned to look out the window.

"I saw Zach take you out on the jet ski. Did he kiss you?" She asked.

"Oh god, can we not talk about this right now?" I asked.

She laughed, "I'm just asking."

"No, he did not. So please don't ask me anymore." I said almost in tears again.

"Okay, I won't. But I think he's pretty dumb if he didn't." She said as I turned to look at her.

She just smiled at me and knew that my heart was broken.

The next week at school I didn't talk to anyone and I avoided Zach at all costs, and Gabriel avoided me in study hall when I tried to apologize to him.

I needed to get out of my head, so that weekend I decided to start running again, and I ran down to the lake. Billy wasn't there, but I said hi to the ducks and sat there for a few minutes to catch my breath.

On my way home I saw a boy hobbling with his bike, and when I got closer, I noticed that it was Billy.

"Billy? Are you okay?" I asked as I ran up closer to him.

He didn't say anything to me.

I ran in front of him and noticed that his bike was all torn up, and then I looked up at him.

"Oh my god, Billy are you okay?" I asked.

There was blood everywhere, dripping from his head and his legs.

"I think I need to go to the hospital." He said as he collapsed into my arms.

<h1 style="text-align:center">Chapter 8: Bidi Bidi Bom Bom</h1>

He was freaking heavy and I knew couldn't walk him back to my house, and yes, this was before cellphones, so I didn't have a way to call anyone. So, the only thing I could think of to do was to leave him by the lamppost while I ran back home to get my mom.

"Mom! Mom!" I yelled as I ran into the house with blood all over me.

"What? Oh my god! What happened?" She screamed as she saw the blood.

"It's not mine, it's Billy's and he's hurt really bad. We have to go get him!" I cried.

My mom grabbed her purse and her keys, and we drove to the lamppost where I left him; he was still there.

"Billy, can you hear me?" My mom said as she snapped her fingers at him.

"He's hurt, not deaf," I said.

"I swear to god Lindsay I don't need your bullshit right now. Go get the cellphone from the glove compartment." She ordered.

Ok, well, she had a cellphone, but it was like one of those Zach Morris, *Saved by the Bell* phones.

"Billy, I'm calling an ambulance." My mom said.

"No please don't, my parents will kill me." He said as he clung to her tee-shirt.

"Ok, well, then I'm driving you to the hospital, Lindsay help me pick him up and put him in the back." She said.

We had just gotten a brand-new Ford Excursion SUV, so there was plenty of room.

"Lindsay, sit back here with him and make sure he doesn't pass out." My mom said as I climbed in the back seat next to him.

He grabbed my hand and I tried to comfort him; he looked like he was in so much pain.

"It's going to be okay; you're going to be okay," I said to him.

He looked at me and tried to smile.

"What?" I asked.

"I was listening to the mixed tape you made me." He said.

"Oh, finally, huh?" I laughed.

"I really like it, and I like that Dep—" He tried to pronounce it.

"Depeche Mode?" I asked.

"Yeah, them. They're pretty cool."

"Well, I'm pretty cool, so—" I said, trying to joke around.

"You are the coolest girl I know." He said as he gasped in pain.

"What did you do?" I asked.

"I was going really fast on my bike and a car came out of nowhere, so I overcorrected and crashed my bike into a ditch."

"Ouch, do you think you broke something?" I asked.

"I don't know, I've never had anything broken, well, except for my heart." He said as he looked at me.

I didn't say anything, but I did grab my disposable camera that was in the back seat.

"Smile!" I said as I took a picture of us together that would later be called a "selfie".

"Really?" He asked.

"I have to remember this day forever," I said with a wink.

We finally got to the hospital and they immediately rushed Billy back into the ER while my mom and I sat in the waiting room.

The hospital was able to get Billy's parent's contact information and called them. They couldn't tell us his condition because we weren't family, but we waited for hours until his parents showed up.

They didn't seem concerned at all, they looked more annoyed than anything like Billy inconvenienced them in some way. It hurt my heart.

We found out through his parents that Billy had a broken wrist, ribs, and had to get stitches in his forehead and knee, but he didn't have a concussion, so they were going to send him home.

I saw the nurse wheel him out in the wheelchair with a sling around his wrist.

Billy's parents were getting the car and I asked my mom if I could say goodbye before we left.

"So, you're going to have a pretty sick cast huh?" I asked playing around.

"I guess so." He said as he looked down at his sling.

"Maybe you should try not rocking out so much to Depeche Mode next time," I said as started walking away.

"Hey, Lindsay!" He yelled.

I turned around to face him.

"Thanks for helping me today." He said.

"Any time. Oh, and um, I'm going to be the first one to sign your cast, okay?" I said with a wink.

"Of course." He said as he smiled back at me.

"I'm really proud of you today Lindsay." My mom said as she held my hand.

"Whoa, I definitely need to capture this moment," I said as I took a picture of her holding my hand.

The next day was my mom's birthday, August 31st, a true Virgo. My dad, who was commuting from Miami to Tampa on the weekends was home to take us all out to dinner to celebrate. We had the best time and for us to all be together again really meant a lot. It was hard not having my dad home a lot, but I'm sure it was even harder for my parents.

That night I was getting ready for bed when I heard my mom yell, "Lindsay get in here!".

What the hell did I do now?

I went into my parent's bedroom and the TV was on and it was breaking news.

"Princess Diana was in a really bad car crash in Paris." My mom said as she watched the TV with concern.

I, along with the rest of the world, was obsessed with Princess Diana. Her clothes, her attitude, and her newly found independence inspired me.

"Do you think she's going to be okay?" I asked my mom as I watched the footage of the black sedan in the Paris tunnel.

"I don't know; it's pretty bad." She responded.

"Can I stay up to watch?" I asked.

"Only for a little bit longer, but you've got school in the morning." She said as I sat on her bed and watched the coverage.

It wasn't long before the reporters cut back on and said that she had died.

That was the first time I had felt grief for someone I didn't even know, but I wasn't alone. The whole world tuned in to watch her funeral as if we all knew her in some sort of way, and we were all grieving. I felt empathy for the brothers who lost their mom because it felt like I lost my mom too.

"This part is always so sad." P said as she watched Prince William and Harry walk behind Diana's casket.

"That's a weird thing to say," I said as I looked at her.

"Sorry, how are you holding up?" She asked me.

"Okay, I guess. It just sucks. You live your whole life and then you just die."

"I think that's the point. It's what you do in this life that matters. Look at the legacy that Diana left behind and look at how many people she helped. That was her life's purpose. Was she taken too soon? Probably, but look at how many people's lives she affected in just a short time here on earth. It's pretty incredible. She was pretty incredible."

"I want to leave a legacy like her," I said wiping the tears from my eyes.

"I don't have any doubt in my mind that you will Lindsay", she said as she hugged me.

I was starting to get used to having P around, even though it still annoyed me that she would pop in and out and that I still had no idea who she was, but she was comforting and always there when I needed her. Maybe she was my fairy godmother.

The next day at school, our history teacher assigned us a biography project where we had to write a paper and do a presentation on someone alive or dead. I, of course, chose my inspiration, Selena. To be honest, the movie had recently come out and I was obsessed with her and her music, so I thought it was the obvious choice.

I worked incredibly hard on that project, more than any other, probably because it was something I was interested in, and I had the opportunity to be creative.

I decided I was going to do a video presentation of me pretending to be a Biography Chanel host discussing the life and career of Selena and then acted out by me, of course.

I wore one of my mom's bustier, jeans, a paperboy hat, and large hoop earrings. I also learned every Spanish lyric to each of her songs; it had to be as authentic as possible.

Then, on the day of my presentation, I decided I was going to dress up in the same outfit and perform a medley of her songs in front of the entire class.

I could hear the gasps and whispers as I walked in the front doors of the school that day. I ignored everyone and went straight into the classroom with my giant boombox. I slammed it down on the table, pressed play, grabbed my mic, and began to lip-sync and dance around the classroom, just like Selena. Then I played my video and the entire class loved it.

Even my history teacher enjoyed it, but she made me change my clothes as soon as it was over—I was, in fact, in a private Christian school dancing around in a bustier.

As my friends and I were leaving the classroom we saw a group of girls from 10th grade, Zach and G's class, by the water fountain. As soon as we walked by, they began to giggle and whisper to one another.

"Did you hear what Cheyanne said?" Asked Roxette.

"No, what did she say?" I asked.

"I don't know if I want to repeat it." She said concerned.

"Just tell me." I pleaded.

"She was laughing at you and asked the girls if they saw your Selena outfit and one of the girls asked which one of us, and she said the girl with the lip."

I immediately felt my heart sink into my asshole. Ever have that feeling?

For some reason, I felt embarrassed, but I couldn't let my friends know it bothered me.

"She's just a bitch." I said trying to brush it off.

"She really is. I loved your outfit and your presentation." Said Deanna.

"Thank you. You girls save me a seat in study hall. I'm going to the bathroom." I said as I rushed to the nearest bathroom.

I sobbed uncontrollably in the stall. The girl with the lip? Is that what she sees? Is that what everyone sees?

Most of the time, I never thought about my deformity, I guess because I lived with it daily, and most of the people around me treated me like a normal person, that was until someone reminded me of it in the cruelest way.

"What happened?" P asked defensively.

"Nothing," I said as I grabbed toilet paper to wipe my eyes.

"Bullshit. Who made you cry? One of those boys? I swear I will kick their ass!" She said as she started to open the door.

"No! It wasn't them." I said as I started to cry again.

"Who was it?" She asked as she got down to look me in the eyes.

"It was an older girl. She called me the girl with the lip. Is that all I am? Just the girl with the messed-up mouth who will never be normal?" I asked crying harder.

P put her hands on my knees and said, "Look at me, look me in the eyes, Lindsay."

I looked down at her as the tears streamed down my face.

"You are a million times better than any of those kids in there. None of those kids know any of the shit you have had to go through and not one of those kids will ever have the heart that you do"

"But I'm so ugly. I will never be pretty like them."

"They're not pretty. Maybe in looks, but those will fade with time. You are beautiful Lindsay. I know you may not feel like it right now, but you are. Right now, you are in the middle of your journey, your journey alone, but you will get to the other side of this and you'll know that everything you have been through, or going through right now, will be worth it. And trust me when I say, outside beauty can only get you so far, it's what's in here that matters the most. You have always let your true beauty shine through, and don't ever let a dumb bitch's comments dull that gorgeous shine of yours. The beauty in here will always show on the outside, just be patient." She said as she hugged me.

"Thank you," I said as I hugged her back.

That was the moment I realized why P came into my life—I needed her. She was comforting, always listened to me, and never judged me, and for some reason, I knew we could relate to one another.

"Now let's wipe those eyes and I want you to show me which bitch said that about you." P said as she took my hand.

We peaked our heads into the classroom, and I pointed her out.

"There she is that's her in the green sweater," I said.

"I got you." She said with a wink as she pushed me into the room.

I sat down next to G and he asked me to borrow my notebook. I slid it to him without making eye contact because I knew he could tell I had been crying. I could see him writing in it as he slid it back over to me and mouthed "read it". The note said:


*Are you okay? You look like you've been crying. Let me know if you need anything.*

*Love,*

*G*

I slid my notebook back over to him with a note:


*I'm fine but thank you for asking and I will let you know if anything comes up* 

*Love,*

*Linz*

He looked over at me and smiled at me which I thought was a little weird because the last time we spoke to one another he stormed off. I guess we were friends again.

As soon as study hall was over, all of the kids ran out of the class and headed down the stairs to the lunch hall. Dee and Roxette were asking me about the note G passed to me in study hall when all of a sudden, we heard gasps and bursts of laughter. I looked over the railing and saw Cheyanne looking over her shoulder at her busted jeans.

"What happened?" I asked a student.

"Cheyanne slipped and fell and busted her pants; you can totally see her underwear."

I thought about what P had said and I knew she had something to do with this.

I saw Cheyanne run into the bathroom, and unfortunately, with all of my crying, I forgot to go to the bathroom, so I went into the same one.

I could hear someone crying in the stall and I knew who it was. Instead of basking in the glory of revenge, I felt sorry for her instead. So, I knocked on her stall door.

"Are you okay in there?" I asked.

"Go away!" She said crying harder.

"Listen, I saw what happened. Let me know if you need anything." I said.

"Do you happen to have an extra pair of pants?" She asked.

"I do!" I said as I reached into my backpack and grabbed the jeans, I wore for my Selena project.

"Oh my god, you're a lifesaver!" She said as she opened the stall door and saw me holding the pair of jeans.

"Oh, it's you." She said as she put her head down.

"You can return them to me whenever," I said as I handed her the jeans.

She started crying, "Thank you. I was so embarrassed. Everyone saw my underwear. Have you ever been that embarrassed before?" She asked.

"More times than not, unfortunately," I said as I turned to walk away.

"Hey, you're Lindsay, right?" She asked.

"Yes, I am."

"Thank you, Lindsay. You're really sweet." She said as I smiled at her and said, "I know." And walked away.

I could have chosen to let her go all day in total embarrassment, but I chose to be kind in hopes that she will remember my act of kindness and choose to pay it forward—and to stop being a total twat.


That weekend was our National Volleyball Tournament; it was pretty much just all of the private schools playing against one another for a little trophy.

I was personally excited because Zach and G were on the boy's team and I got to watch them play all weekend long.

"Hey Linz, what are you doing for fall break? G and I are going back to the lake and wanted to see if you'd like to come?" Asked Zach.

Any other time and I would have been able to go, but my family decided to plan a trip to Miami and Key Largo for the break.

"I would love to, but the fam and I will be out of town next week, " I said disappointed.

"Aw man, maybe next time." He said as he spiked the volleyball with his beautiful body.

My JV volleyball team played well and ended up getting second place in the tournament, and I even got a trophy; the only sports-related trophy I would ever receive.

The next week my mom piled my brother and me into the Excursion and drove from New Port Richey to Miami where my dad lived temporarily in a small apartment.

We were thankfully not staying there, but instead, stayed in a nice hotel on South Beach. Miami was hot and loud, but the energy there was unmatched. Everyone was tan, beautiful, and happy. If it were my choice, I would have stayed in Miami for the entire trip, but unfortunately, we were also going to Key Largo.

So, you know that Beach Boys song "Kokomo"? Yeah, Key Largo isn't anything like that song.

It didn't help that the hotel we stayed at had a sewage problem that backed up into the pool. Literal turds were floating in the pool next to my brother. I decided to hang by the bar ordering virgin daiquiris and people watched.

My dad had a brilliant idea to book a glass-bottom boat tour, thinking we would all enjoy it, but as soon as I boarded the boat a seagull took a giant shit on my head. Some people may say a bird shitting on you was good luck, but as a thirteen-year-old, it was the end of the world.

My mom, of course, found my embarrassment to be the highlight of her trip and couldn't stop laughing at my misfortune, but she did go to the boat bar and ask for some paper towels.

"I think our captain is drunk. He's over by the bar wasted." My mom said when she came back with the roll of paper towels.

"Are you sure it's the captain?" My dad asked her.

"Oh yeah, I'm positive." She said still laughing at me.

Then, we were all called down to the bottom of the boat which was all glass so you could see the ocean. It was really beautiful, and we were all enjoying watching the fish when all of a sudden, we felt a thud and were all jolted forward.

"Did we hit something?" My mom asked my dad.

"It sure felt like it." He said as he added, "C'mon, let's all go back up to the deck."

As we were walking up the stairs, we could see the captain throwing buckets of water off the side of the boat.

"Um ladies and gentlemen, we, unfortunately, hit some coral on our journey, so we need to head back to the dock as soon as possible." Said the captain over the loudspeaker.

"That's just fucking great." My mom said as she grabbed her wine glass.

Meanwhile, I kept thinking maybe it was finally it, maybe I was finally about to find out how I die; you know, after all those missed calls, maybe this was how I go.

It took us three hours, crawling on the ocean, to get back to the dock with my mom saying, "We're all going to drown" the entire time, but we finally made it back on dry land.

I guess the bird shitting on my head was good luck after all.

Needless to say, I couldn't wait to get back home.

When I went back to school the next day there were all sorts of buzz and whispers when I walked into the classroom.

"What's going on? Why is everyone whispering to each other?" I asked Roxette.

"The school is going to let us have a homecoming this year. The homecoming court, the dance, the whole nine yards, and it's only for 8th-12th graders. They are announcing the homecoming court nominees this morning." She said overly excited.

Why didn't I know about this? I was usually in the know about all of the happenings in school, but I did just get back from out of town.

"How do you get nominated for homecoming court?" I whispered back to Roxette.

"Shhhh ladies, I am about to pass out the ballot for homecoming court. Please keep your voices and opinions to yourselves. Only Jesus should know what you're thinking right now, got it?" Ms. Green asked.

My heart started racing for some reason, it's not like I was going to be nominated for something like homecoming court, that kind of shit was for the pretty popular girls.

Ms. Green handed me a ballot and my eye immediately went to the 8th-grade nominees.

"Holy shit! I was nominated?" I yelled.

"Ms. Young! Principal's office, now!" Yelled Ms. Green.

Not again.

I had to explain to the Pastor how it was wrong for me to put holy in front of shit, but I didn't even care I was so excited that I was even nominated for homecoming court.

When I saw my friends at lunch, they were so excited as was I.

"We have to go dress shopping!" Squealed Deanna.

"Um, aren't you forgetting something? What about the dates? We have to have dates to homecoming. Lindsay, who do you want to go with?" Asked Roxette.

Oh shit, with all the excitement with my nomination I didn't even think about who I wanted to go with or who would even want to go with me.

As I waited for my mom to pick me up after school, I heard G's voice.

"Lindsay, I have something for you!" He yelled from across the parking lot.

He ran up to me in what it looked like to be slow-motion. The way his olive skin glistened in the Florida sunlight and how his athletic body moved with ease as he ran towards me.

"Hey! I meant to give this back to you, but I just haven't had the chance." He said as he pulled my notebook out of his backpack and handed it to me.

"Oh thanks, I've been missing this," I said as I reached for it and touched his hand. It felt like a bolt of electricity rush through my body.

"I really liked the story you wrote in there." He said with a wink.

"You read my story?" I said as I slapped him with the notebook.

"Yeah, I made a few changes-nothing too major." He said laughing.

"Linz, c'mon!" My mom yelled from her car.

"I gotta go, thanks for giving this back you thief," I said as I walked away.

When I got into the car, I felt someone grab the door.

"Hey Linz, can we talk tomorrow? I have something I need to ask you." Asked Zach.

"Uh yeah sure," I said as I looked at my mom.

"Hi, Zach." My mom said trying to be polite.

"Hi, Ms. Young. I'll see you tomorrow?" He asked me.

"Yeah, see you tomorrow," I said as I buckled my seat.

"What was that about?" My mom asked.

# Chapter 9: Tubthumping

"I have no idea. Everyone's acting all weird about homecoming, which I got nominated to be on homecoming court." I said as I pulled out the nominee list and handed it to my mom.

"You did? Well, that's exciting. Have you thought about who you want to go with?" She asked.

"No, I'm sure no one would want to go with me," I said.

"Oh, now I'm sure there are plenty of people who would love to go with you." My mom said smiling.

"We'll see," I said rolling my eyes at the thought of someone wanting to take me.

"Oh, your dad and I are headed out of town tonight and won't be back until next week. Your grandma is coming to watch you and your brother while we're away." She said.

This would come as a surprise to any normal family, but my parents did this kind of stuff frequently since my dad started working in Miami and commuting back home every weekend.

"Where are you going?" I asked.

"Oh, just a business trip, we'll be back on Sunday." She said as we pulled up to the house.

I saw Billy on his bike waiting at our garage.

"How's your broken body?" I asked him with a smile.

"It would be better if you signed my cast." He said with a wink.

"Is that why you came over here?" I asked him.

"No, it's one reason, but I also came to ask you something else." He said as he handed me a sharpie.

"Oh, and what would that be?" I asked as I began to write on his wrist cast.

"Well, my school is having a homecoming dance and I wanted to see if you would like to go with me?" He asked.

"Like a date?" I asked as I handed him back his Sharpie.

"No, the last time I checked that wasn't going to happen, but just going as two friends. We can dance, have fun, what do you say?" He asked me.

"That sounds nice, I'd like to, when is it?"

"December 2nd." He replied.

"Really? Saturday, December 2nd?" I asked frustrated.

"Yeah, why? You already have plans?" He asked.

"Ugh, that is the date of our school's homecoming."

"Your school is allowing you to have a homecoming?" He laughed.

"Yeah, they finally agreed to it and I got nominated to be on the court." I looked at him annoyed.

"Why do you say it like that? That's a pretty big deal."

"I know it just sucks, I'm sorry," I said as I put my hand on his shoulder.

"It's cool, I had to shoot my shot." He said as he grabbed his bike.

"Do you want to stay for dinner? I'm sure my mom won't mind."

"No, I have to get home and make dinner for my parents, but thanks for asking." He said as he hopped on his bike.

"How do you ride that thing all broken?" I asked laughing.

"I'm not broken, just brokenhearted." He said as he smiled and peddled off.

Why was he so annoying?

"Linz, what did Billy want?" My mom asked as she was making dinner.

"He asked me to his homecoming dance, but it's the same date as my homecoming dance," I said with a sigh.

"Well, that's frustrating. Why don't you ask him to your dance?" She asked.

"I don't know, maybe," I said as I grabbed my backpack and headed into my room to do homework.

"OMG, homecoming court? That is such a big deal!" P said as she jumped and slammed her body on my bed.

"You're a little too big to be doing that you know?" I asked her as I went back to doing my homework.

"So, who do you want to go with? I have my favorite, but I want to know yours." She said as she put her face in her palms and stared at me until I turned around.

"You know you are so freaking annoying, right?" I asked her with a heavy sigh.

She just stared at me until I answered her question.

"Fine. I really don't know."

"Omg yes, you do! I know you better than you know yourself." She gasped.

"Oh really? Then who do I want to go with Miss Know It All?" I asked.

"You want to go with G. I saw the way you flirted with him today." She said with a huge grin on her face.

"What? Flirt? No, I did not. We were just talking." I said as I turned back around to my homework.

"What if he asks you; you would say yes, right?"

"Of course! I'm not an idiot. He is the most popular guy at school."

"And the cutest." P added.

"If you like him so much why don't you go with him?" I said sarcastically.

"I would if I could." She said looking at my CD collection.

"I'm not going to worry about it because he's not going to ask me anyway."

"Now, you don't know that. You are a catch little Lindsay, and any boy would be so lucky to have you as his date—just as long as it's not that Zach guy." She said as she stopped to look at me.

"What's wrong with Zach?" I asked her.

"I don't know, I just think there are better options for you, that's all." She said as her eyes got big like she knew something I didn't.

"I've got to finish this homework before my dad and grandma get here."

"Cool, cool, but keep me posted on what happens, k?" She asked.

"K," I said with a giant smirk.

The next day my parents left for the airport extremely early, so my grandma took my brother and me to school.

Everyone was abuzz about homecoming at our morning chapel assembly, that was until the Pastor put a stop to the commotion by picking up little Bobby Brown and shaking the devil out of him-literally.

"Now listen, I am not on board with this homecoming nonsense. I think it's just an excuse to invite evil into your souls, so that is why it will not take place on church grounds. Your teachers will let you know where this sinister congregation will take place, but just know there will be rules you must follow, or you will be asked to leave. No short dresses or dresses that show any female body parts, there will be no dancing of any kind and no secular music."

You could hear were the awes and boos.

"If ya'll don't like the rules, we can cancel this fiasco at any time, got it?" He yelled.

"Maybe I should go to Billy's homecoming instead," I whispered to Deanna.

"Ms. Young, do you have something you would like to share?" Asked the Pastor.

"I was just whispering to my friend here about how much I love Jesus," I said with a smile.

"I'm sure you were." He said as he continued talking.

Deanna and I looked at each other and laughed because I'm pretty sure there was something in the Bible about not lying in a church.

When I got to study hall, I saw G's hand go up as he began to wave me over to him.

"I save you a seat." He said as he patted the chair next to him.

I suddenly began to get nervous and I couldn't figure out why; I was never nervous around him before.

"I saw you get called out in chapel; you rebel." He said laughing.

"You know me, never following the rules," I said trying to sound cool.

Ugh, what was I doing?

"I like that about you." He said with a wink as he got out his notebook.

My face started to get hot and red as G started to write something in his notebook.

He slid me a note that read:

*Can we talk after school?*

I wrote back:

*Yeah sure, but it has to be right after our last class because my grandma is picking us up.*

He read my note and nodded his head.

Oh my god, I was freaking out. What if he was going to ask me to homecoming? I had to play it cool, but I was dying on the inside.

The rest of the day seemed to last an eternity when the last bell finally rang. I ran down to the basketball court where G and Zach usually hung out until their moms came to pick them up.

But when I got there I was immediately pulled over by the bleachers.

"Hey Linz, you got a second?" Asked Zach.

"Yeah, but just a second," I said looking over at his shoulder to see if I could see G.

"So, you know homecoming is coming up and I wanted to see if you wanted to go with me?"

To be honest, I wasn't listening to him because I was focused on finding G, so I said what any other person would have said when they weren't paying attention.

"Uh-huh," I responded.

"Really? You'll go with me?" He asked.

"What?" I asked as I came back to reality.

"You'll go to homecoming with me?" He asked again, but this time I *actually* heard it.

"Wait, me? You want to go with me?" I asked.

"Yeah! I wasn't sure you wanted to go with me because I heard you wanted G to ask you, but I didn't want to be the one to have to tell you this, but he's taking Amber from our class."

I'm sure if you listened hard enough, you could have heard my heart shatter into a million pieces at that moment.

Amber? G never even talked about her, and I never saw them together, so it came as a huge surprise to me that he wanted to go with her.

"So, what do you say? Will you be my date for homecoming?" Zach asked for the third time, this time grabbing my hands.

I wanted to start crying, but not because Zach asked me to homecoming, but because I realized at that moment who I truly wanted to go with, but it was too late, he didn't want to go with me.

'Yeah, I'd love to." I responded with a halfhearted smile.

"Great! We'll talk later about the details, but I can't wait." He said with a wink and ran off.

I ran outside to find my grandma when I heard G call my name.

"Lindsay, where were you? I've been looking all over for you." He said as he ran up to me.

"You know, don't bother, I already know—you are taking Amber to homecoming."

"What? Who told you that?" He asked shocked.

"Zach told me. He and I are going to homecoming together."

"What? When did he ask you?"

"Just now, listen, Amber's really nice, and I'm sure we'll all have a great time—I've got to go, my grandma's here."

"Lindsay, wait!" He yelled as I got into the car.

"Grandma, let's go," I said as I buckled up.

"Don't you want to talk to that boy?" She asked.

"No, I just want to go home," I said as I could feel the tears well up in my eyes.

When we got home, I could hear my grandma talking to my mom about me.

"Yeah, she said Zach asked her to homecoming—well, I guess she said yes." My grandma said to my mom.

I was so confused and didn't know what to think, everything just kind of happened so fast, and the only thing I wanted to do is put my head in my pillow and cry.

"Zach? Really?" I heard P ask as she appeared from thin air like she always did.

"Please don't lecture me; I've had a really bad day and I don't need to hear your shit," I said as I put my head back in my pillow.

"Well, smothering yourself won't do you any good. Do you even want to go with him?" She asked.

"No, well, maybe, I don't know. The one person I wanted to go with chose to take someone else, so if the most popular boy in school asks you to Homecoming, you say 'yes'."

"I'm sorry Linz, boys are stupid, and it won't get any better when you're my age, unfortunately. They just turn into adult-size idiots."

"You're being really helpful, thanks," I said sarcastically.

"Just go with Zach and try to have a good time, but if he tries anything, I'll kick his ass." P said.

I laughed, "I would love to see you try to kick someone's ass. You're the girliest…omnipresent being I've ever seen."

"Listen, looks can be deceiving; I've been known to beat a bitch's ass a time or two." She said laughing.

"Have you thought about what you want to wear?" She asked very enthusiastically.

"No, I've been so busy with all of this "date" drama that I haven't even thought about it, and I've never been to a dance or homecoming before—I don't even know what to wear'" I said frustrated.

"Oh, have no fear, if there is one thing I know—it's fashion! You are going to be the most beautiful girl there; I promise you that!" P said confidently.

I wish I had the same confidence that she had in me.

My grandma told my mom everything that happened while she was away, and she wasn't very happy that I was going to homecoming with Zach.

"I thought you liked Zach?" I asked my mom on our way to the mall to go dress shopping.

"He's perfectly fine, but he was not who I thought you were going to go with to homecoming." She said sounding disappointed.

"Well, he asked me, so we're going together," I said trying to end the conversation once and for all.

When we got to the mall, we headed straight for the department store where I spent hours trying on dresses.

"You don't like any of these?" My mom asked frustrated.

"No, none of them are me," I said equally as frustrated.

"Well, let me go look again." My mom said as she stepped out of the fitting room.

Then I heard a knock on the door.

"Yoo! Hoo! It's P; I think I found the perfect dress." She said as she slid the dress through the crack in the door.

It was a yellow, spaghetti-strapped, corseted, tulle ball gown—it looked like a modern version of Belle's dress in *Beauty and the Beast*.

When I put it on, it felt like it was made just for me, it fit perfectly.

"P, this dress is ama—" I said as I walked out of the dressing room and she was gone.

Then my mom walked up and gasped.

"Lindsay, you look so beautiful! Where did you find this dress?" She asked.

"Someone helped me find it," I said as I twirled around in it.

"Is this it? Did you find the one?" My mom asked.

"Yes, this is it!" I said yes to the dress.

The following day, Shirley had asked my mom and me to help Zach pick out his tuxedo. I was nervous because I hadn't seen Zach since he asked me, and I was I worried that he would change his mind about asking me to homecoming.

When we arrived at the tuxedo shop, I wasn't prepared to see G there too, shopping for the tuxedo he was going to wear to homecoming with his date who wasn't me.

"Hi, Linz." He said as he stepped out of his dressing room looking so cute in his tux.

"Hey," I said trying to play it cool and act unbothered.

"What do you think?" He asked.

"Think of what?" I responded.

"Of my tux!" He said laughing as he spun around in it so I could get the full view.

Now he was just being cruel.

"It's nice," I said as I walked up to Zach.

I looked over at G and he put his head down and walked back into his dressing room.

The following weeks before homecoming were the busiest, and Zach and I were constantly writing notes back-and-forth to one another about Homecoming and how we were so excited.

"You guys are going to be the cutest couple there," Roxette said to me after class.

"We are not a couple," I said trying to downplay Zach and I's interactions with each other.

The day of homecoming finally arrived, and I was so excited and nervous at the same time.

My mom took me to get my hair and make-up done that morning and my dad had hired a limo driver to take all of us over to the venue.

I heard everyone arriving at our house one-by-one, and then I heard Zach. It was time to make my grand entrance. Living in Florida, two-story homes were rare, so I couldn't have my *She's All That* moment, but I made some jaws drop when I entered the foyer.

My mom greeted me first as I handed her my purse to hold onto until all photographs were taken.

Then, my eyes met with Zach's as he ginned so big.

"Look at you, Precious. You look beautiful." He said as he nervously slid a corsage onto my wrist.

"Ok, you two get together so we can take your picture." My mom said taking full control over the photo-ops.

As Zach and I were getting blinded by the flash photography, I saw Gabriel and Amber walk in together. My heart sank. That should have been me on his arm and not her. I was so hurt and confused, but I tried so hard to push those feelings down so I could enjoy the moment. I was going to homecoming with the most popular boy in school after all, and *he* asked *me*.

We all got together for a group picture, which was hella awkward because I was sandwiched in between Zach and Gabriel. This continued on our limo ride to the venue as well. No one spoke to one another the entire ride there, which was weird because Zach and Gabriel were best friends, but they weren't saying a word to each other and you could feel the tension.

"Look, there's Billy's high school," Zach said as he pointed to the school which was located directly across the street from the Country Club where we were having our homecoming.

"Oh yeah, they are having their homecoming tonight too," I said as I looked out the window to see if I could find Billy.

"Oh really?" Zach asked.

"Yeah, he asked me to go and I couldn't since they are both on the same day," I said still looking.

"He did, did he?" Zach said curiously.

When we arrived at the venue there was yet another photographer waiting to take our picture. While Zach and I were getting our picture taken, I looked over at G and he had the saddest look on his face like he was about to cry. I should have been the one looking on the verge of tears, not him.

When we walked into the ballroom there were balloons and banners everywhere, and even a DJ which I was pretty sure was not allowed, but it was super cool.

We all found our seats and of course, I was sitting directly next to Gabriel.

Gabriel helped me into my seat and when I looked up, I saw Zach and Amber making a weird face.

"Thank you," I said softly to G.

"I'm going to get us some punch," Zach said as he stormed off.

G sat down and was messing with his napkin.

Amber decided she had to go to the restroom, so it was just us sitting at the table.

"This is really fancy." G said messing with the cutlery and glasses.

I chuckled a little.

He leaned in closer to me and whispered, "You look beautiful tonight."

I looked over at him and into his eyes and I was speechless.

Then, he was about to say something else when Zach walked up with our punch.

"Did I miss anything?" He asked as he sat down next to me.

"No, we were just talking about how fancy this whole thing is," I responded looking over at G who looked annoyed at Zach's presence.

"Alight everyone in their seats, it is time to announce this year's homecoming court. If you were nominated, please line up in the front." Said Ms. Green over the microphone.

"Well, I guess that's us," I said to our table as I started to get up.

When I did, G got out of his seat to help me and Zach immediately jumped up and said, "I got it, man. You worry about your own date."

I immediately felt an awkward twinge in my stomach and could feel the tension between them.

Zach held out his arm to guide me to the front of the room to line up. The nominated girls were on the opposite side as the nominated boys so when our names were called, we would join each other in the center of the ballroom.

As I was standing there nervously waiting for my name to be called, I looked over at the boy's side and I saw Zach and G arguing.

"And from the 8th-grade class, please give an applause for Lindsay Young." Said Ms. Green over the microphone as I made my way to the center of the ballroom floor. I look next to me and I was alone.

# Chapter 10: Closing Time

I heard gasps and a crowd of people rushing outside the venue. When I looked over to where the boys lined-up, I noticed Zach and Gabriel were gone.

I Picked up my ball gown and ran outside. I pushed my way through the crowd to see Zach and Gabriel fighting one another. Well, more like Zach punching the crap out of G. I looked around and no one was stopping them, so I had to do something.

I threw myself on top of Gabriel and threw my hand out and yelled "Stop!"

"Stop fighting each other, please!" I yelled with tears in my eyes.

I looked down to check on G, "Are you okay?" I asked him.

"Oh, you're going to see if he's okay? What about me?" Zach said with adrenaline still pumping from the fight.

"You're not the one bleeding on the floor," I said as I helped G up.

"No, because I'm not a pussy like him," Zach said with a laugh.

"No, you're a true asshole. Lindsay, I'm so sorry." G said as I handed him a tissue for his bloody mouth.

"Sorry for what? Why are you guys fighting with each other?" I asked confused.

"Tell her the truth or I will." G said looking at Zach.

"The truth about what? Will someone please tell me what's going on?" I asked looking at them both.

It was silent and then G started talking.

"I wanted to take you tonight, I even asked your mom if it was alright, but Zach found out, and before I could ask you and he asked you first."

"But you told me he wanted to take Amber," I said looking at Zach.

"I made it up. But he's lying to you too. G, why don't you tell her the whole truth?" Zach said.

G was quiet.

"Fine, I'll tell her since you can't. Over the summer, G and I made a bet to see which one of us would be able to get you first. To be honest, it was a little more difficult than I thought it was going to be, but I guess I won."

Tears streamed down my face as I stood in between them.

"So, that's all I am to both of you, some stupid bet?" I asked sobbing.

"You totally just quoted *She's All That* just now," Zach said laughing as he turned his back.

"Is this from *She's All That*?" I said as I punched his jaw so hard that he fell to the ground and all the students laughed at him.

I picked up my dress and started to run off.

"Lindsay, wait!" G said as he grabbed my arm.

"Don't touch me. Don't even come around me again, do you understand?" I said as I shoved his hand off me and ran to the golf course to be alone.

I fell to the ground on the 9th hole and put my head in my hands to cry.

"I will kill them." P said holding a putting iron.

She sat down next to me and I collapsed in her arms sobbing.

"I'm so sorry Lindsay." She said as she held me.

"I'm so stupid, here I thought they liked me, but it was a stupid bet this whole time. I should have known they would never like me, how could they? I will always be the girl with the broken smile." I said as I cried harder.

"Well, I told you that Zach was trash, but I did have high hopes for G, he has a really great butt." P said trying to make me laugh.

"Ew, you're like 25," I said as I looked up at her.

"Aw, that is the nicest thing you've ever said to me." She said holding her heart.

"Listen Lindsay this is the moment I've been waiting forever since I crashed into you. This pivotal moment where I am supposed to give you some life-changing advice that will have an indelible impact on your life forever, so here it goes—men ain't shit."

"That's your advice? I can kind of figure that out for myself." I said frustrated.

"From now until you're my age you are going to realize this pattern, but I'm going to let you in on a little secret, there is one person who you are going to fall head over heels in love with." She whispered.

"Finally, you tell me something good. When do I meet this person?" I asked her.

She smiled big and said, "You already have."

"Who is it? Tell me!" I said impatiently.

"Point." She directed me.

I pointed my finger as she took my hand and pressed it against my chest.

"It's you. You fall madly, head over heels in love with yourself, and when you do, everything in your life falls into place. Lindsay, you are going to realize how truly beautiful you are, inside and outside. And yeah, you aren't like anyone else, but you know what? That makes you even more beautiful and it sets you apart from the rest because no one can ever be you. Own who you are, love who you are, be confident in the human being you are becoming and will become. You are going to accomplish so many wonderful things and there is going to be so much love in your life you won't even know what to do with it."

"What I do now? I just wait?"

"Oh my god, just be a teenager. All teenagers are awkward and so damn impatient. Just have fun and try to enjoy it. You know a wise man once said, 'Life moves pretty fast, if you don't stop to look around, you could miss it'".

"Did you just quote Ferris Bueller?" I asked smiling.

"What? He's like my hero." She said as she hugged me then turned to look at me with a huge grin.

"I heard that someone else is having a homecoming tonight too." She said as she looked over at Billy's high school.

"I think you should go make a little cameo." She said with a wink.

"You know what, you're right!" I said as I stood up in my big poofy dress and gathered up the bottom.

"That's my girl! You go have fun and don't do anything I wouldn't do!" She yelled as I started running toward Billy's school.

When I walked into the gym there were so many students dancing, laughing, having fun, but how was I ever going to find Billy in that crowd of people?

I scanned the room looking at every single person, but I couldn't find him. Maybe he decided not to go.

I was about to give up and walk out when I felt a tap on my shoulder. I turned around and there he was standing there smiling.

"Don't you look beautiful?" He said looking me up and down.

"You decided to come after all." He said as he took my hands.

"Wanna dance?" He asked as I nodded my head yes.

I wanted nothing more but to let loose and have fun, especially after the night I had.

We were dancing, laughing, and having so much fun. Then the song switched to a slow song, K-Ci and Jojo's *All My Life*.

Billy pulled me closer and put his hands around my waist as I put my head on his shoulder. It was like there was no one else in the room and everything that happened to me that night didn't matter. I was dancing with my best friend and that was all that mattered to me at that moment as I started to cry.

When the song ended, Billy looked at me and saw that I had been crying, so he whispered, "Do you want to go somewhere quiet and talk?".

I nodded m head "yes" as he took my hand, and we went to the football stadium to sit on the bleachers.

"What happened tonight?" He asked looking deep into my eyes.

"Exactly what you said would happen. Zach is a total douchebag. Do you know that he and G had a bet to see which one could get me to go out with them first?" I asked disgustedly.

"That is typical Zach. When we were in school together, every girl that I liked, he tried to go out with before I could even ask them. He always must be first in everything, no matter whose feelings he hurts. I'm sorry that happened to you, you don't deserve that. I can kick his ass for you if you'd like?" He asked as I snort laughed.

"Did you just snort?" He asked laughing.

"Billy, can I ask you something?" I said seriously.

"Sure, ask me anything."

I paused then asked, "Why do you like me?"

He got quiet and then looked at me and smiled, "Because, I think you are the prettiest girl I've ever seen, and you're funny and kind, well, kind to others, not so kind to me."

I play pushed him and laughed then asked him, "You think I'm pretty even with my scar?" I asked.

"Especially with your scar. That's what makes you so cool." He said as he traced my scar with his finger.

"Thank you," I said softly as I looked into his eyes as his eyes pierced through mine as our bodies got closer. I closed my eyes, and I could feel his soft lips on mine. My first kiss.

It felt like it lasted forever and then we both opened our eyes and laughed.

"Yeah, no, we should just stay friends." He said laughing.

"Yeah, it's like kissing my brother," I said busting out laughing.

"Best friends?" Billy asked me.

"Best friends," I said as I hugged him tightly.

After we danced a little bit longer, I had Billy take me home.

When I arrived at my house, I was greeted by my entire family who was sitting in the front room all with serious looks on their faces.

"Am I in trouble?" I asked.

"No, why do you think that?" My dad asked me.

"Because I had Billy take me home tonight," I said fessing up.

"What? Billy? Was Billy at your homecoming?" My mom asked.

"It's a long story, I'll tell you later. So, why are all of you in here?" I asked as my stomach began to churn.

It couldn't be good news, it's never good news.

"I was telling everyone that I have been offered a new job." My dad said excitedly.

"Really? Are you moving back here?" I asked even more excitedly.

"No, it's in North Carolina." My mom said unenthused.

"North Carolina? But, what about my school, my friends? I'm in 8th grade, do you know how hard it is to make new friends in 8th grade? When are we moving?" I yelled as I started to cry.

"Next month." My mom said so nonchalantly.

A shitty night just turned into an even shittier night.

"I hate this! Why do we always have to move!" I yelled as I ran into my bedroom.

Not a few seconds went by as I heard a knock on my door. It had to be P, but she never knocks, she just popped up out of thin air.

I opened the door as I tried wiping the tears out of my eyes. It was my mom.

"Can I come in?" She asked.

I motioned her to come in as she immediately sat on my bed.

"Daniel told me what happened to you tonight. If I were there, I would have pulled Zach's testicles right off."

My mom certainly did have a way with words.

"I should have known, I should have seen it coming, from Zach especially. I didn't see it coming from G." I said as I started to cry again.

"G? What did G do?" My mom asked shocked.

"He and Zach had a bet to see which one would be able to get me to go out with them first."

"That little asshole! Do you know before I left on the trip with your dad, he came up to me and asked me if he could take you to homecoming? That's why I was shocked when you said you were going with Zach, but that little bitch was in on it too. Well, I'm sorry that happened to you. Did you at least get a good punch it?" My mom asked.

"I sure did," I said with a smile.

"That's my girl. Now, I know moving is not ideal, but it's what's best for our family. Your dad can't keep commuting back-and-forth to Miami every weekend. Plus, he really seems excited about this new job—will you try to make it work?" My mom asked.

"I'll try. It's just that I'm always the new kid and I'm always having to explain myself and why the way that I am. It's frustrating."

"I know it Linz, but I know one thing about you it's that you are one of the strongest, most resilient girls I've ever known, and there is no obstacle too great for you to take on. I know you've had to be brave your entire life, from the first moment I met you, but you just have to be brave a little bit longer. You amaze me every single day. When I look at you, I see nothing but the best parts of me inside of you—you're everything I wished I could have been at your age. You are the kindest, strongest, smartest, strong-willed child, and I've always been terrified that you would resent me." She said as she started to cry.

"Resent you for what, mom?" I asked.

She put her hand on my mouth and said, "For this."

"Mom, I never think that at all. I do sometimes think that you wish you had a normal daughter, one that doesn't have so many issues."

She laughed and hugged me.

'And what would be the fun in that?" She said as she laughed and hugged me tighter.

"I love you so much Lindsay Paige, no one will ever love you as much as I do." She said as she kissed my forehead.

"I love you too," I said as we sat there and hugged one another.

"Are you off school for New Year's Eve?" My mom asked me.

"Yeah, I think so, why?"

"Your dad wants to take us and maybe Maggie to Universal Studios to celebrate New Year's Eve there." She said rolling her eyes.

"That would be fun, I'll ask Maggie if she wants to go."

"You're not mad at her?" My mom asked.

"No, I'm mad at her brother. I'm sure she had no idea what he was up to." I said as I grabbed the phone in my room.

"Make it quick, I think your brother wants to use the internet." She said as she left.

I called Maggie and she apologized profusely for her brother's actions towards me. I don't know why she was apologizing since it was her brother who was being the douchebag, but I accepted her apology and she agreed to go to Universal Studios with us.

I was thankful that our school was on holiday break and I didn't have to see anyone after the events during homecoming, especially Zach and G.

My mom said that G called our house but asked for my brother. I'd like to say I couldn't believe neither he nor Zach have even attempted to apologize to me, but I wasn't surprised. They had no regard for me or my feelings at all, so it made moving a little easier.

Christmas was uneventful and bittersweet since it was going to be our last one in Florida. I never thought I would miss not having a white Christmas, but I was going to miss it terribly.

I also had not seen or heard from P since my homecoming and I was starting to think that she was gone forever. Everything in my life was changing and I had no control over anything; I know that sounds overly dramatic, but I was a twelve-year-old girl, everything was dramatic.

When we arrived at Universal Studios, my dad passed out our entry tickets to each of us.

"Dad, did you get an extra ticket?" My brother asked.

"Extra ticket? Who else is coming?" I asked.

As soon as the words left my mouth, I heard, "Hey guys!"

Fuck, it was G.

I immediately grabbed Maggie and yelled, "Bye, we'll meet you guys later!" as I nearly pulled her arm out of her socket as we ran away.

"What is he doing here?" I furiously asked Maggie.

"I have no idea." She said as she looked just as confused as me.

"Well, I am going to avoid him at all costs today. C'mon, let's have fun!"

And we had the most fun all day, that was until we decided to ride The Hulk rollercoaster.

"There you guys are! We've been looking for you all day." My brother said as he and G walked up to us as we waited in line.

I turned my back and started talking to Maggie. Then I felt a tap on my shoulder.

I turned around and gave G a look.

"Hi. Can we talk?" He asked.

"I don't have anything to talk to you about," I said trying not to engage in conversation.

"Well, I do. I want to apologize to you for everything thing that I did. I am so sorry I hurt you, that was never my intention." He said as he pleaded.

"What was your intention? Because you did hurt me. I wanted to go to homecoming with you. I thought we were friends, but I guess I was wrong about that just like I was wrong about Zach being a nice guy." I said as I turned away from him.

He grabbed my shoulders and turned me around to face him.

"I wanted to go to homecoming with you and not because of some stupid bet. When I made that bet I was the new kid in school and I heard Zach was popular, so I just went along with it, but then I really got to know you and I really started to like you. I even wrote you a letter in your notebook."

"What? When?" I asked shocked.

"In study hall, I asked to borrow your notebook and gave it back to you. I'm guessing you never read the letter." He laughed.

"No, I didn't even know," I said shocked.

"I know I really messed up, but I hope you can forgive me." He said as he held out his arms for a hug.

I smirked and grabbed his hand and pulled him to the front of the rollercoaster.

"You scared?" I asked him with a smile.

"Not at all." He said with a wink.

We had the most amazing day riding rides, eating, laughing, and then we all gathered to watch the ball drop for the new year.

The countdown began as G folded his hand into mine and smiled. As the countdown went to one, the fireworks went off and G pulled me close to him as he kissed me.

As we pulled away, I tried to regain my balance and said, "Wow, that is definitely not like my brother."

"What?" G asked laughing.

"Long story," I said realizing what I just said and laughed.

G still holding me, whispered, "I can't wait for this new year."

As soon as the words left his lips and seeped into my ears, I started to cry.

"What's wrong? Was it something that I said?" He asked.

"No, I have something to tell you," I said sobbing.

"What? What is it?" He asked concerned.

"My family and I are moving in a few weeks."

"Moving? Where?" He asked.

"North Carolina," I said trying to control my tears.

"Well, North Carolina is not too far away, and my grandparents have a house there in the mountains, so I can visit you. It's going to be okay." He said as he hugged me.

As I looked over his shoulder, I noticed a familiar friend giving me a thumbs-up behind his back.

I pulled away from G and said I needed to go to the restroom.

I ran up to P and hugged her.

"Where the hell have you been?" I said frustrated.

"Um, you are not the only job I have okay?" She said in her sassy tone.

"There is so much I need to tell you," I said trying to think of where to begin with everything that has happened.

"I have something to tell you too, but you go first." She said as we sat down.

I told her everything that happened at homecoming, Billy, my kiss with G, and then I finally told her that I was moving to North Carolina.

"I know, and that's why I have to tell you that I can't come with you." She said.

Her words were like daggers to my chest; even though she was a major pain in my ass popping up out of nowhere all of the time and causing drama, I was going to miss her.

"Why?" I asked.

She smiled and took my hands, "Look bitch, I told you I have other things to do besides be your sexy fairy godmother, okay? Plus, you don't need me anymore. I have seen you flourish over these past few months; you can handle anything that comes your way."

"Will I ever see you again?" I asked her.

"I think so." She said with a wink.

"Pojo!" My mom yelled.

"Yes?" Both P and I answered.

"Your name is Pojo? Wait…" I said as the lightbulb went off.

"You're me? What kind of weird *Shining* bullshit is this?" I asked her.

"It's about time you figured it out. I was dropping hints like crazy, and then I was like, I know I was not *that* dumb." She said laughing.

"But you're so pretty," I said as I observed every inch of her face.

"Don't you mean, you're so pretty?" She asked me.

"How are you even here right now?" I asked her.

"I think when you died during your surgery, someone (pointing up) thought you probably needed a little help. But now, my work here is done, so I'm off to being fabulous elsewhere."

"But I have so many questions," I said not wanting her to go.

"And all of the answers you seek are right here." She said as she pointed at my heart. "Listen to this and nothing else. You're going to be great! Oh, and stay away from boys named…nope, you know I can't tell you that" She stopped herself.

"I love you Lindsay you're going to do great things, trust me," She said with a wink.

I heard my mom calling for me and turned around, but when I turned back, P was gone.

"You're awfully quiet." My mom said on the way back home.

I couldn't tell her I had a lot on my mind, like how I just got kissed by the cutest boy in school, I had to say goodbye to my imaginary/maybe real friend who was also myself, or that I felt like my entire life was changing in an instant, so I just responded with, "I'm just tired, that's all."

The next few weeks felt like they flew by. I had to tell all of my friends at school I was moving, G and I were technically going out, but it was only temporary, and there was still one person I hadn't told that I was leaving and I kept putting it off.

"Why did you want to meet me here?" Asked Billy as he looked out over the lake.

"I have something to tell you and something to give you," I said.

"Why tried that already." He said implying that I wanted to kiss him.

"Very funny. Billy, my family is moving to North Carolina." I said as I observed his face.

"Really? When?" He asked.

"Next week," I said cringing.

"Next week? And when were you going to tell me? When you had already moved?" He said frustrated.

"I know, I'm sorry, I've been putting it off because you're the one I'm going to miss the most," I said honestly.

"There you go, breaking my heart yet again. Damnit Lindsay I am going to miss you so much." He said as he started to cry.

"I'm going to miss you too. You are my best friend, Billy, and you always will be. Here, I made you this." I said as I handed him a mixed tape.

"It has all of my favorite songs on it and when you start to miss me, you can play it and think of me."

"It better have some Depeche Mode on there." He said laughing as he wiped the tears from his face.

"I love you." He said as he took me in his arms and held me.

"I love you," I said as I laid my head on his chest.

We stayed at the lake for hours lying on the grass just being together.

The night we left we were greeted by our friends to give us a final farewell. We hugged, we cried, and we said our final goodbyes, and as we pulled away, I couldn't help but reflect on how much my life had changed and how I changed over that year. I also gave Zach the finger as we drove by just for good measure.

I was excited and nervous about the next chapter in my life, but I knew I had what it took to take on anything that came my way.

And, while we were at a stoplight on our way out of the city, I looked over at the car next to us, a gorgeous red Acura NSX, and I swear I saw Pojo as she gave me a wink as she drove off.

**THE END.**